TRAITOR ANGEL

The Angelkiller Triad

Book One
ANGELKILLER

Book Two
TRAITOR ANGEL

Book Three
DOOM ANGEL
(not yet released)

TRAITOR ANGEL

H. DAVID BLALOCK

 SEVENTH STAR PRESS

Cover art and illustrations: Matthew Perry
Cover art and illustrations in this book copyright © 2012 Matthew Perry
& Seventh Star Press, LLC.

Editor: Amanda DeBord

Published by Seventh Star Press, LLC.

ISBN Number 978-1-937929-73-2

Library of Congress Control Number: 2012950454

Seventh Star Press
www.seventhstarpress.com
info@seventhstarpress.com

Printed in the United States of America

First Edition

To those who have believed in me,
and those who think I'm just a figment
of their imaginations.

Thanks for the inspiration!

PROLOGUE

In the beginning, there was a war.

Humanity had just sprung from an afterthought in the great Mind of the Master when His first creations, the angelic hordes, began to vie for control over the new creation. In time, Mankind would come to think of those who rebelled against God's intent as the Dark or Fallen Angels and those who conformed to their Master's Plan as the Angels of Light.

The war raged for centuries, with neither side gaining advantage until the Dark took a daring step and opted to involve Men in the struggle. As a result the Dark gained an unwitting ally, the very creation for which the combatants struggled.

Forbidden to harm Man by the Master Himself, the Angels of Light retreated and the forces of the Dark won by default what they had coveted for so long. But the victory came with an unexpected cost.

In order to retain their prize, the Dark found it had to deceive Man into believing he had fought for the right side, the side that upheld the Master and His Plan. The Dark had to convince Man he had fought for the Light, and that the Light won.

That deception continues to this day, but there are those who have learned the truth and fight to right the heinous wrong wreaked on Humanity, to defeat the Dark and manifest the real victory of the Master: the bringing of Light into the world. These fighters originally were few, and by Grace were given long life and wisdom. They received the name Angelkillers for their faithfulness to the Conflict. Each built a cell of followers until, over the years, a new force appeared. Called simply The Army and sworn to secrecy out of necessity, they lived in the shadows and struck at The Enemy when the opportunity arose. Eventually, an Angelkiller would be raised to the station of Knight, whose power was second only to the Angels. When a situation was particularly critical to the Conflict's advancement, a Knight would be dispatched to tip the balance. For more than one Knight to appear was historical. For three to appear at a time indicated events of apocalyptic proportion.

Jonah Mason was an Angelkiller and head of one of the cells of the North American Army resistance. For centuries, he had fought the growing secular atmosphere of a nation losing its soul to the materialistic and cynical influence of The Enemy. Most recently, he and his group had faced down the Minion Azazel, a minor demon in the employ of a mysterious Enemy agent known only as Andrael, at the request of the head of a global corporation whose name was Dorian Azrael. There had been reservations about working for Azrael, about siding with The Enemy even if it was against another Minion. Mason had overridden those reservations, and in so doing had involved them in an intrigue they began to suspect involved much more than just the rebellion of one Minion against another.

The most disturbing part of this event, however, was not that Mason had to face a Minion, but that three Knights had appeared, ostensibly to support him.

Though one of the cell's number, Harold Martin, was hospitalized from an earlier encounter with the Minion, and two others, Stephen Overguard and Janice Meeker, were not to take part in the final battle, Mason drew the Minion out and faced it down with the aid of the Knights. However, in so doing they unwittingly awoke in John Tripp, Mason's oldest ally, a previously unsuspected problem. Tripp, unbeknownst to the rest, witnessed the appearance of a Seraph at the end of the battle during the Minion's exorcism. His Puritan background rose up from its long-forgotten place in the back of his mind, and he became obsessed with seeing it again, no matter the cost.

Mason himself was faced with a choice after the battle. It became clear the reason so many Knights had appeared was not just because the Minion had to be put down, but because

Mason, an Angelkiller, had made a deal with Azrael, an agent of The Enemy. The Knights were not impressed by his reasoning or excuses, and Mason now faced an ultimatum that would strike to his very soul.

1

The dawn was just breaking as Jonah Mason sat on his porch, trying to put in order the events of the past few days. The chill of the early morning air stung his face, but its clean taste helped him focus. The slight creaking of the glider rocker drifted across the lawn to rebound against the oak and hickory woods that began sixty feet from his front door. Between him and the little two-lane road that ran three hundred feet away, the white gravel drive split those woods. He watched as a doe trotted out of the forest to pause, head high, and look at him before continuing across the drive, followed by two spotted fawns. Overhead he heard geese honking and somewhere a squirrel chittered its displeasure at being awakened. He stretched his long legs out in front of him and leaned back into the rocker. Anyone passing on the road would get a glimpse of a very tall, well-built man with dark hair, dressed in nondescript clothing, sitting on his front porch. An ordinary picture with an extraordinary secret.

As bright as the morning was, Mason's mood was dark. The fight with Azazel had been brief, for all it might have seemed to take an eternity, and he himself had played practically no part in its climax. Besides bringing the Minion to the battlefield, he'd been little more than a spectator, looking on as the real work was done by the Knights. At one point his own humanity had reduced him to blindly cowering in terror behind the Knight named Jaelon, and he shuddered to think what might have happened had it not been for her interference.

The Knights appeared and events had changed; he saw that now. Certain failure had turned into success. Without their presence, Azazel would surely have left him a shivering, insane hulk there on the darkened grounds of the city park. It was sobering to see that Azazel could have done exactly that anytime he wanted, but didn't. The true danger of dealing with the Minion only now dawned on him.

"Mason."

He looked up to see Jaelon leaning toward him. She had done something to her hair, probably Janice Meeker's idea. He hadn't ever really looked at her as a woman, but her sudden appearance let him do so, if only for a moment.

She was average height, with dark auburn hair usually fixed in her native Pictish manner now done in the modern style. Her eyes were a startling bright green, evenly set above high cheekbones. She wore the same kind of garment the other Knights wore: a utilitarian, nearly uniform-like khaki device with an abundance of pockets. Unlike the others, she wore it well. She wasn't strikingly beautiful. More handsome than beautiful. But definitely more female than he recalled.

To her left stood Antonius Malthusan, arms crossed and glaring at him. He was a big man, better than six feet tall and heavily built. Before becoming a Knight, he had been a Cypriot mercenary and had seen service in the Crusades. He was ever so slightly graying at the temple and the stubble of a beard threatened to burst through his face, darkening the skin. Mason noticed more scars on the man's arms than he remembered. Malthusan had grudgingly accepted the fact that Mason was the leader of the cell. His opinion of that was no secret. He felt that Mason's deal with Azrael was against everything their side in the Conflict stood for. Mason knew Malthusan considered him a traitor and only held himself in check because of Jaelon, who they early on saw as the ranking member of the Knights.

The last of the three, Krato Populus, sat on the hard porch with his head against the wall, apparently dozing. Mason knew better. Populus might be the least garrulous of the Knights, but very little escaped his attention. The man's slight build was deceiving, as he knew full well. Populus was wiry and agile, in the style of an Olympic gymnast. His hair, curly and dark, fit his Grecian olive complexion. He had a keen mind that adapted quickly to changes in their situations, analyzing and directing alterations to their strategies unerringly.

That they had approached without him realizing didn't surprise or bother him. His discomfort at their initial appearance had given way to an easy acceptance and welcoming. Even he, who had fought in the Conflict for longer than he cared to remember, felt safer in their company than alone. Looking at them, he was beginning to feel a camaraderie he hadn't felt for a very long time. Was it because they were natives of a time closer to his own? Was it because of the air of confidence and surety they exuded? After all, they had each actually seen the face of the Master. They absolutely *knew* the truth of what they did. How could they not?

"What is your next move, Septimus Vernus?" Jaelon asked.

He frowned at her, uncertain what she meant. She never used his real name unless they were alone, away from the rest of the cell. After the battle with Azazel, they had told him his deal with Dorian Azarel, in their eyes, was the worst kind of mistake, a bad example of a lack of faith. No matter what his rationalization might be, working *for* The Enemy was working *with* The Enemy. It had taken the three Knights confronting him there, still on the battlefield, to imprint that fact on him. Pleading his case, making the excuse he was doing it to protect his team, sounded weak in his own ears now. He would always remember the look on Jaelon's face when she had asked that question: "Where is your faith?" Faith in the others, that they could cope with whatever they needed with the same courage and determination he had used. Faith in his cell, that it could operate effectively without him if necessary. Faith in the Master that He would provide for their needs, no matter the consequences.

In spite of everything, and perhaps to allay his mounting fear, they revealed the Master knew his heart and accepted what he had done was out of concern for others and not himself. Then they told him.

He could either accept promotion to Knight or his involvement with the Conflict was over.

In the back of his mind, he had both hoped for and dreaded this decision. Being given the honor of becoming a Knight was the dream of every member of The Army. To see the face of the Master, to stand in His Presence, and to finally know without any shadow of doubt everything he had done for so long was right, true, and vindicated...

On the other hand, to be removed from the Conflict, to find the peace he had often dreamed about? To never again have to be responsible for anyone but himself, to finally sleep soundly, unconcerned with the intrigues of an unending war? Who wouldn't want an end to the unending stress, the constant fear, because fear was always part of his life. Long ago, even as a humble soldier for Rome, he had come to accept that fear and learned to deal with it. Though it had never completely left him, it had only faded into the background, remaining a nagging annoyance.

He had no concern about what might happen to him if the Master excused him from the Conflict. Retired Army veterans were given the remainder of a natural lifespan. He had done his best to serve the Master since being recruited, and what he'd seen in just the last few days had removed any doubt what his fate might be.

So, was she talking about the ultimatum they had pronounced to him, or was she referring to the next step in dealing with Dorian Azrael?

"Azazel is just the tip of the iceberg, Vernus," Jaelon said, as if reading his thoughts. "The files he had you retrieve from Panama must be the key to something much more dangerous, more far-reaching than his influence."

She was referring to the files on a USB drive he and Tripp had recovered from one of Azazel's companies', Catalina Industries, branch office. In order to draw the Minion out of his safety zone, they had to cooperate in some less-than-honest activities. They had tricked an employee into giving them access to the company computers. Once they had the files, they had arranged for the meeting that led to Azazel's downfall.

Mason nodded. "There's something there we're missing."

This was painfully obvious to all of them and had been on their minds as they returned from the park after the confrontation with Azazel, lost in their own thoughts, contemplating what they had seen. Overguard and Meeker, who had been sent to check on Martin at the hospital, met them at the house shortly before noon. Tripp was very late turning up. Mason worried about that, but his attention was drawn to the more pressing problem of what to do with the information they had retrieved from Catalina Industries. Catalina was simply one branch of a mega-corporation called Andlat Enterprises headed by Dorian Azrael.

Thankfully, Malthusan brought Martin to him soon after, probably because he had complained to Jaelon about needing the man for his computer expertise. Even though Mason was centuries old, and had faced at least three Minions in his life, computers remained a daunting mystery to him. Give him a quiet day, a good cigar, and a book to read and he was happy.

Martin might still be in a wheelchair, but his spirit was unfazed. He sped into the office with the energy of a man half his age, nearly running over Mason's foot in his excitement to find out what was on the USB drive that Azazel had thought was worth his life. He wheeled in front of Mason's workstation and went to work.

They discovered the files were a gateway to Azrael's network of corporations, a back door to the intricate web of servers that controlled his empire. It was little wonder Azrael had come to them to stop his Minion from stealing them. But, there was an unexpected discovery waiting for them in those files.

The Minion had not been working directly under Azrael. There was a middle man, someone named Andrael. It was then that Jaelon had suggested they adapt the I/O sets to allow the entire cell to enter that virtual reality interface, so they could use their whole resources against whatever resistance they might encounter.

"Thanks to you," Mason went on, "Martin is here and working on that. If anybody can figure it out, he can."

Jaelon nodded and smiled. "I am sure." She looked around and motioned to Malthusan, who went inside the house. "Are you coming in for breakfast?" she asked Mason.

"In a bit," he promised.

She followed the big man inside. Silence settled over the porch and Mason watched the trees sway in the morning breeze. Dandelions were starting to bloom in the yard near the treeline. He made a mental note to do something about that.

"You cannot put it off forever, you know."

Mason nearly jumped. He'd forgotten Populus was there.

"What?" he asked.

"You will have to make a decision soon," the Knight said.

"Yes, I know," Mason replied. "Soon."

Populus unfolded himself from the floor and stretched. He gazed at the woods. "Beautiful. I can see why you like it here." He breathed in and exhaled. "It is too bad you can no longer stay, now that Azrael knows where you are."

Mason didn't answer that. Truth to tell, he had been avoiding that particular problem. He was just beginning to realize how attached he had become to this place. It had served him well for over sixty years. His Haven. His refuge. No longer safe, because of his own sloppiness in letting Azrael find it.

He frowned. How *had* Azrael found it, after all? That was a question that needed to be answered as well. As far as he knew, he was the only person aware of its existence before the Minion's black sedan had come down that drive. He had been so careful to keep this place a secret. No one else knew of it.

No one but Tripp.

He shook his head. Tripp was his oldest, most trusted ally. They had been together for better than four centuries, since New England. There was no way Tripp would betray him to The Enemy.

And yet, that day he came back from seeing Martin at the hospital, the door wards had been down and Azrael and Tripp were in the house. What had they been talking about before he got there?

"Time for coffee," Populus said, interrupting his train of thought.

Mason found he was glad of it. How could he suspect Tripp of being unfaithful? It was ludicrous. Just a product of his unease about making the decision Jaelon wanted.

That must be it.

2

The office was well appointed. A state-of-the-art computer system took up the whole of one wall. Doors fed the room from two of the other sides, while the last wall was occupied by a bookshelf crammed full of tomes whose titles whispered in languages modern, ancient, and forgotten. The computer desk chair stood empty beside the man working the machine. His wheelchair shivered as he worked, running his hands from one control to another. His shock of unkempt blonde hair, testimony to his Teutonic ancestry, matched the hint of mustache above his lips.

Harold Martin paused in his work, frowned, and scratched his head. They had been lucky enough to get access to Catalina Industries' computer infrastructure, but the intricacies of its internal security measures were giving him fits.

He had decided to concentrate on the system branch

tagged for the mysterious identity labeled "Andrael". Neither Mason nor any of the Knights said they recognized the name, which only deepened the mystery. That this Andrael had never before appeared in angelic literature or tradition meant it was part of a previously unknown hierarchy, which bordered on the impossible, or it was the name of a human agent, like Jenkins. However, unlike Jenkins this Andrael was probably not directly possessed. Martin reasoned Andrael was a high-ranking lieutenant in Catalina Industries, someone very close to the top. Since Azazel had been under him in rank that meant Andrael was the real mover behind Dorian Azrael's hiring them.

Martin shook his head. What could possibly be in those files that Azrael was so afraid of? And why would someone already subservient to him gaining access to them be a problem? Then again, it could be what they always suspected: simply an ambitious underling trying to pull a coup by blackmail. It was the constant infighting among The Enemy that was The Army's best weapon after all. Their conceit partnered with their paranoia often generated opportunities to strike places that would otherwise be invulnerable.

Martin picked up the modified I/O set and clamped it around his neck. Amplifying the data stream interface had helped him access deeper protocols in the matrix infrastructure, helping him find hidden files and fragments of deleted material he could reconstruct almost at will. Using his improvements to bypass firewalls and breach blocked servers, he had explored all but the most central data on Catalina's network. Besides the odd pornography and a couple of amateurish hacker attempts, he found nothing out of the ordinary for a business the size of Catalina Industries.

He was down to the core files, the heart of the company. Whatever Andrael wanted must be there, but what an odd way to go about getting there. Why not just use a Catalina machine? Nothing he found so far would have stood up to even the determined efforts of someone with half his skill and resources. Surely a Catalina machine fit to the company network would have the necessary protocols built in to access the core. Generate a false ID, rotate the IP, and reroute the query, and a hacker could be in and out in a matter of seconds. Sure, the intrusion would be logged, but if it were properly tagged as a company machine the inquiry might go unnoticed for hours, days, or completely. Typically, the further you got into a network the less likely you were to run into security protocols anyway. Individual files might be protected, but the system itself would be open.

So, the core must be where the treasure lies. What would Dorian Azrael keep in his system that he wouldn't want found?

More importantly, why would he? It had to be something he prized, but nothing that would damage him personally. Minions were egotistical but not completely foolish.

Martin logged in, bracing for the initial disorientation. A moment or so later, he found himself standing on the bleak alien landscape of the interface.

Nothing looked natural. Everything that moved did so peculiarly. Trees swayed sinuously. Bird-like animals flew overhead in a haphazard fashion. With an effort, he ignored the way things turned wrongly, the dizzy color shifts, and concentrated on the angelic script seemingly hanging in midair before him. It glowed gently with an undefinable tint that hurt the eye if you looked too long at any one sigil.

He double-tapped the script for Azrael and all sound ceased as he again found himself facing a blank wall.

The wall stretched from horizon to horizon, from the ground to infinity above him. He knew there had to be a way through, but so far the passkey had eluded him. For the umpteenth time, he stepped to the wall and touched its smooth surface. It was like opaque glass, with no visible breaks, cracks, doors, or marks whatsoever. Martin was more convinced each time he got to this point that the key to everything lie just beyond that wall. Back there were the core files of this infrastructure, the coding keys that held Catalina Industries together, and the answer to why Dorian Azrael came to them to handle his "little problem".

He paced the wall for several hundred feet either way, knowing that it was silly to do so. Whatever method might be used to get past the wall would be just as effective where he entered as anywhere else. Of course, there was always the distressing possibility that Azrael himself was blocked access from the core, although that seemed unlikely. Minions cherished control above everything. Martin couldn't see Azrael abdicating control of his own corporation computer system to anyone, much less some nameless IT stooge.

No, there had to be a way in, a way easily accessible to Azrael, something he could do or say or input. What would Azrael use that would never occur to anyone else?

Then a thought came to him. Of course! But, how to input that into the program? It wasn't like there was a button for it.

He pulled back out of the interface and logged off. The real world snapped back around him and he was once again in Mason's office. He reached for his own laptop and booted its web browser. A few seconds' search was all it took.

* * *

Mason's living room was a testament to a life spent more concerned with simple survival than decoration. No pictures hung from its paneled walls. Only two large, high-backed chairs sat in front of the fireplace, separated by a single coffee table. All the furniture would have been more in fitting with a house eighty years older than it was. The hardwood floors were mostly bare, the occasional area rug insufficient to cover them. Old-style electrical fans hung from the ceilings and hummed as they turned. Mason, answering Martin's shout, came in through the connecting door from the kitchen.

"All right, Harold," Mason said, taking a seat. "What's up?"

Martin, his portable PC draped across his lap, rolled his wheelchair around until Mason could see the screen.

"I suddenly remembered something you mentioned once," Martin said. He hit a few keys and pointed at the monitor.

"Lilac?" Mason read.

"Lilac. You once told me you often smelled lilac when a Minion was close."

"So?"

"That's it!" Martin announced triumphantly. "Catalina

manufactures a line of perfumes that includes several variations on lilac. I tried the product numbers, formulae, and the names until I got the right passkey."

"What was it?"

"A combination of all three, actually, but with a place to start and the right software coding, I cracked it in less than three hours."

"Well done," Mason said. "What did you find?"

Martin grinned. "A veritable jackpot. Names, addresses, and a database of financial information for dozens of Azrael's agents."

"Incredible. Any Minions named?"

"Minions and human agents both," Martin nodded. "It's a back door to his entire empire."

"No wonder Azazel wanted it so badly," Mason said.

"With this, we can break the back of Azrael's organization in less than a week," Martin crowed. "From what I have here, it looks as if fully one third of The Enemy's resources would be crippled or outright destroyed. It would be the most significant step toward ending the Conflict since it began!"

"And what would be the cost in human life?"

They turned to find Populus standing in the front door. The Knight looked from one man to the other.

"How can you have been so long in this Conflict and not realize it is more than just a war we can see with our eyes?" Populus said. "We are fighting not just for this generation, not just to win a partial victory. We are fighting to win back the heart, mind, and soul of all Mankind." He stepped through the doorway and pointed at the computer. "If we use this new information to beat Azrael, another will replace him. We gain nothing and may possibly cause undue suffering."

"We cannot turn our backs on this opportunity, Populus," Mason insisted. "It is our duty to take advantage of every chance we get."

Populus shook his head. "It is our duty to *use* every advantage to its utmost, but that does not give us license to forget the cost we might incur."

"So, we figure out how to use this information while minimizing collateral damage," Martin put in.

"Collateral damage?" Populus said. He leaned against the wall and scowled at them. "People are not 'collateral damage', Mr. Martin."

"Wars have casualties," Mason answered.

"This is true," Populus allowed, "but those casualties must only ever be among those who choose to knowingly be part of that war."

Martin huffed in frustration. "Fine words, but not very realistic."

The Knight regarded them thoughtfully for a moment. "This conflict is escalating, gentlemen. You can see it not only in the recent affair with Azazel, but in the increasing tensions and skirmishings in the Middle East. You could say the area once known as Mesopotamia is a crucible for the rest of the world. As goes the Middle East, so goes history.

"Catalina Industries is heavily invested in the Middle East, in case you hadn't noticed. Everything from oil and weapons to coffee and diamonds are funneled through Catalina Industries from there. You said yourself, Mr. Martin, that fully one third of The Enemy's resources are involved. Do you honestly believe The Enemy will allow that to change without a fight? Every resource you cut off will precipitate a need which will be met from somewhere, whatever the cost."

"So, what good does it do us to have this information if we can't use it?" Martin groused.

"Ah," Populus said with a grin. "We do not need to use it to give us an advantage. We simply let Azrael know we have it."

The others exchanged puzzled looks. Populus tilted his head at them.

"Gentlemen, do you not see? If Azrael knows we have this information, he will assume we will use it against him. It is what he would do and the Minions always use their own expectations to gauge the actions of others."

Mason snapped his fingers as the truth hit him. "Azrael will have to take steps to neutralize the perceived threat."

"Thus, any damage done will only be to those who have already committed to The Enemy," Populus finished. "No 'collateral damage.'"

"Wait a minute," Martin interrupted. "In that case, wouldn't Azrael already have rendered this information useless? He knows we have the USB drive."

"I sincerely doubt he has the confidence in your talent we have, Mr. Martin," Populus said. "I am sure he is certain the firewall protecting the core server is enough to keep us out, and the other files we could access represent no real threat."

"Fooled him," Martin gloated.

"Indeed you did, my friend," Populus said.

"Okay, so how do we go about this?" Martin asked.

"I am afraid I will have to leave the details about that to you and Mr. Mason," Populus said. "We Knights are forbidden to engage in intrigues, for obvious reasons."

"Well, we can't do anything until we're secure, and I'm

still working on that," Martin said.

Mason sighed. "Excuse us, then, Populus. Martin and I have some plans to make."

Populus bowed slightly and left the two men to plot.

* * *

Janice Meeker had always wanted to be a part of something special, something really important, and when Overguard came along she got her wish and more.

Being part of The Army was both exciting and terrifying. The things she had seen in the last few days may not have been as impressive as what Mason saw but just to be around them and the Knights was thrilling. Her life before this was little more than a shallow dream, nothing but surviving day to day in a dingy, lackluster world. Her life now was filled with unfolding mysteries, adventures into the unknown, and people whose existence she had never imagined, much less suspected. When she went to bed at night the events of the past few months replayed so much in her head she had trouble sleeping. It wasn't insomnia born of fear. It was anticipation of what the next day might bring.

They spent most of their time now at Mason's house in

rural Tennessee. It was a bit more country than she liked but she understood the need for it. With Azazel dead, the only Enemy agent that knew their location was the one who originally hired them. She knew Mason was already arranging to move their base elsewhere, but with the three Knights staying there she felt perfectly safe anyway.

The Knights fascinated her, especially Jaelon. She knew Jaelon was probably as old as Mason but the woman looked no older than the others, maybe in her late thirties, early forties. What must it be like to live so long looking like that? And what must it be like to have actually seen what she heard the Knights had seen: the face of the Master.

They exuded confidence and surety. Looking at them, you had no doubt they were certain they fought for the right side. There was no doubt in their manner or speech. But there was an unsettling feeling of intolerance as well. She got the feeling, even looking at Jaelon, that they would never give ground on what they believed to be true, no matter what.

She often wondered if they were mortal. They might have received great power but could they still be killed? They could still be defeated, this she knew from conversation with Mason. Immortality might not be one of their traits but death didn't seem to hold any fear for them. How could it, if what was said about them was true?

She wished she could be that certain about things. She wasn't yet thirty, hadn't seen half of what even Overguard had seen, but shouldn't she at least know in her heart how she felt about things? Especially after the time she'd spent with these people.

After breakfast, she found Jaelon sitting on Mason's front porch staring at the woods that surrounded the house. Meeker looked but didn't see anything out of the ordinary in the forest. Malthusan was standing nearby, casually watching them. She didn't really know what to think about that man. She knew he didn't like Mason and he was kind of the muscle behind the Knights, but that was about all. He watched her as she moved toward Jaelon but made no other acknowledgment of her presence.

"Am I intruding?" she asked Jaelon.

The woman looked around at her and smiled. "No, not at all," she said.

"May I join you?"

"Of course."

Meeker stepped up beside Jaelon, who gazed at her expectantly. Meeker stood uncertainly for a moment. Why exactly was she there? Was she looking for something from

Jaelon? Answers? The Truth? Certainty?

"Is there something I can do for you, Miss Meeker?" Jaelon asked.

Meeker got her first real look into Jaelon's eyes and for a moment couldn't catch her breath. All her life she'd heard the old saw that the eyes are the windows of the soul. She never took much notice of that until just then. Jaelon's eyes shone from a depth impossible. Meeker felt like she was looking into a bright green abyss filled with a whirling white mist.

Jaelon blinked and the vision was gone.

"Wow," was all Meeker could say.

"I am sorry," Jaelon said. She looked away. "I was communing when you came up. I forgot."

"Communing?"

Jaelon nodded, clasping her hands together and touching her mouth with them. "How do I explain this?" She stood and sighed as she motioned for Meeker to sit. "Please."

Meeker took a seat on the glider rocker.

"Have you ever wondered how a person becomes a Knight?" Jaelon began. "What it takes?"

"Well..."

Jaelon smiled at her. "There is a price to be paid, Miss Meeker. A price few people understand." She paced for a moment without speaking. "When I was twenty-seven years old, my father and mother were killed by Roman soldiers. I spent the next three years in a dungeon at Londonum, then a year in slavery traveling through Gaul.

"You cannot imagine what that kind of life was like, Miss Meeker. Our masters did not feed us. We lived off what vermin we could find near the camp. While our masters lived in tents with cushioned floors, dry and comfortable, we slept in the mud. The horses had it better than we did." She stopped, probably realizing the bitter tone that crept into her voice. After a moment to collect herself, she smiled at Meeker and went on. "I escaped shortly before our party was to board a ship on the southern coast of Gaul. I found out later the ship was lost in a storm off Malta. I still believe that was the first sign I was chosen." She looked briefly at the sky and that long look took her. She shook her head as if to clear it and turned back to Meeker. "I had no sponsor as you did. I slowly found myself drawn into the Conflict through natural reaction to what I considered injustice. I traveled extensively. Somewhere along the way I came to the attention of a man named Clement, a priest in a small village of Sardinia."

Meeker was held spellbound by Jaelon's account. She could tell the woman was abbreviating heavily the centuries of her life but Meeker was reluctant to press her about details for fear it might interrupt her narrative.

"Clement had already recruited Populus and Malthusan, but shortly after we met, Clement was killed." Jaelon stopped and Meeker watched the memory flit across the woman's face, leaving more than sorrow in its wake. Meeker suspected there had been something other than recruiter and recruited between Jaelon and Clement. "After his death, we bound together and went to work against The Enemy wherever we found it. It was nearly three hundred years later that we encountered a dying Knight."

Meeker gasped. "I thought... well, I always assumed..."

"That we cannot die?" Jaelon finished. She shook her head. "Like the rest of The Army, we are long-lived but not immortal. We are just as susceptible to death from accident or injury as anyone else."

"Oh."

"The Knight was an ancient named Cyrus, a Sumerian. I never found out how he was wounded. I got the impression he had encountered a Minion unexpectedly and was unprepared. Malthusan told me later he spoke of a Minion calling itself Pazuzu and that they had been battling for a very long time. Kind of a personal grudge, if you will." She paused to think for a moment. "At any rate, Cyrus gave me this talisman." She produced a small bauble from inside her blouse, pendant from a silver chain. It glittered green and red as she turned it over in her hand. "He told me it was magical." She laughed to herself. "Magical. If it really was, he would not have died."

"May I?" Meeker asked, holding out her hand.

Jaelon pulled the chain over her head and dropped the item into her outstretched palm. It was a beautifully wrought tiny silver bull with emeralds and rubies worked into an intricate design along its sides.

"It's beautiful," she said, handing it back to Jaelon.

Jaelon gazed sadly at the trinket before slipping it back around her neck and tucking in into her blouse. She pressed it against her chest and closed her eyes briefly. Meeker watched her lips move for a few moments, then Jaelon opened her eyes and sighed.

"It was a few weeks later that I had my Vision," Jaelon went on.

"Vision?"

"It is different for everyone," Jaelon explained. "The revelation. An epiphany of who you really are. For me, it came shortly after Cyrus passed.

"I was in my chamber preparing for bed, when I caught

my reflection in the basin's water. Until that moment I had never wondered at my own longevity, why I had not succumbed to old age as my compatriots had. Life then was much different than it is now, Miss Meeker. You are blessed with plenty in all things. Survival is almost guaranteed for you. We lived by the strength of our arm and wit. Today, in this country you need only ask to receive what we shed our blood to obtain."

"We still have people starving," Meeker protested. "We still have poverty, disease, famine..."

Jaelon smiled grimly. "My dear, I lived through the dark days of the Black Death. You have not seen squalor and filth until you see bodies, unburied and rotting, stacked on pyres and burned like cordwood. You have not seen fear until you have watched people fleeing disease-ridden cities or burnt out towns, fired by authorities desperately trying to stop the contagion.

"I have lived through many wars, fought in most. I have scars you cannot see. You do not understand despair until you see women and children bereft of their men by conscription of their husbands and sons. You do not understand horror until you see the shattered and dismembered bodies on the battlefield drenched in blood..."

Meeker shuddered at the images springing to mind.

"Please. Enough. I get the point."

Jaelon lapsed into a thoughtful silence. Meeker sat thinking about her words, unable to shake their impact. The woman was right. She would never be able to understand what Jaelon had gone through, but was that so bad? Wasn't it the dream of every generation to leave a better, more prosperous world to their children? Jaelon had suffered, that much was evident, but Meeker found it hard to believe her suffering had been in vain. Meeker didn't know that much about this great Conflict. She hadn't been a part of it that long. Still, she knew that the world was a better place than when Jaelon was born. War was now generally avoided. The idea of crimes against humanity had been born of the atrocities of the twentieth century wars. Mankind in general had grown wiser. Maybe not by much, but some. And wasn't that the point? Wasn't that the goal? To awaken Mankind from his ignorance and shine the light of Truth in the world? Wasn't that what they fought and died for? To reveal the Great Deception holding Mankind in bondage to The Enemy?

Maybe Jaelon couldn't see the progress made because of who she was. A Knight's perception of the world must be so different, so geared toward perfection, that they saw only flaws in men. Could that be why they fought so hard? Wouldn't it wear on them? Discourage them over time?

"This vision," Meeker said. "What was it like?"

Jaelon's face turned toward the woods so that Meeker could only see her profile, but there was no mistaking that long look she saw earlier.

"It was a touch," Jaelon began, "a gentle caress to soothe my sorrow. I felt it move within me, healing wounds I never knew I had. I felt a warmth, as sunlight on my skin, though it was long past nightfall. I remember closing my eyes and a peace came over me such as I never experienced before. Suddenly I felt a presence, and when I opened my eyes..." Her voice broke at the memory but a smile spread over her face. "There are no words to describe it."

Meeker's heart quickened. She sensed rather than saw a glow in Jaelon's demeanor. The woman was re-living a landmark event in her life, an event as powerful and evocative now as then. Meeker felt a need to reach out and touch her, as if touching Jaelon while she remembered that vision might let her share just a little of the joy reflected in the Knight's face.

Jaelon turned as Meeker's fingers met her forearm, the light in her visage slowly fading as she returned to the present.

"When I commune, I relive that experience, Miss Meeker. I feel that warmth and comfort. I revel in that peace. Afterward,

I am renewed. In body and mind and purpose, I am reborn."

Meeker was startled to find a tear on her own cheek. The yearning she felt was gone but not forgotten.

She hoped someday she, too, would share in that vision.

3

John Tripp sat looking vacantly into his glass of water. It didn't matter how much he tried, he couldn't get that image out of his mind.

Seraph.

Such an inadequate word, so unbelievably insufficient to describe the vision that left him stunned and shaken for hours.

He had meant to help Mason because he didn't completely trust the Knights to protect his friend. Oh, he had no doubt they would handle Azazel. It was whether Mason would survive while the Knights were doing their "magic" that bothered him. He had left Overguard and Meeker in the van over their objections and made his way into the park just as Azazel, clothed in the body of Michael Jenkins, met Mason. The idea was to get Azazel to agree to an exchange: the files for a binding oath Azazel would not use information he had about their cell against them. To most people, giving their word about something meant very little. Too many people made and broke promises without a single thought. Minions, on the other hand, once sworn were bound, for the power behind the oath was eternally watchful.

Minions feared very little as much as they feared the attention of their superiors and when they swore an oath it had to be by the authority of someone higher ranked. Mason knew this when he made that a condition of the trade. It was almost a given Azazel would double-cross them because of that. Tripp was sure the Knights knew that as well. For all their posturing and impressive presence, they were simply human after all.

Tripp had not always thought so. Before he saw the Seraph, he had been as awed by the Knights as the rest of his cell. Afterward, he felt nothing could ever compare. He could still see it whenever he closed his eyes.

It was as much a feeling as a vision. To relive it brought back the wild terror and joy he felt almost as vividly as when he first caught that glimpse there in the park. In many ways, he supposed he was fortunate it had only been a glimpse, that he had not been standing by Azazel when the Seraph appeared. He was certain seeing it in its entirety as the Minion had would have left him insane or dead. As it was, he was thrown to the ground, experiencing in that brief instant before blacking out what it must be like to stand before the Master, for that is where the Seraph is continually stationed.

He remembered being stripped to the soul, every word spoken, every action taken, everything left undone or unfinished bared to its sight. He had never felt so helpless, so completely vulnerable, yet at the same time so protected. He was terrified in a way he had never known, a soul-searing fear that held him paralyzed, while at the same time a deeper part of himself soared with a wild, uncontainable delight. His mind writhed, simultaneously and desperately accepting and refusing what he could not, would not, wanted and yearned for. Even now, he broke out in a cold sweat as the memory sent chills through him. Tears came unbidden, his heart raced, and his tongue shriveled. In spite of all that, he gladly tortured himself with the memory. The unfettered happiness that came with that vision far outweighed the guilt and terror.

All his life he had been taught about the majesty and beauty of angels. Paintings, frescoes, and statues from every civilization and time tried to capture it. He knew now that nothing, absolutely nothing, could do justice to the reality. Not even the nearly infinite canvas and incomparable ability of human imagination, with its ability to surpass the physical and touch the spiritual, was equal to the task.

Once more he felt the initial shock and confusion, not unlike what he felt when experiencing being shelled in the trenches at Ypres during the Great War. It began as a shudder deep within, like that concussion, and then he found himself temporarily blinded by a radiance immeasurably more pure than sunlight. When his sight did clear, what he saw lasted only a couple of seconds, but it was branded permanently on his soul.

Angelic icons, products of human imagination, make mundane that which is in reality ineffable. For those few moments, his entire existence was laid bare before the incorruptible. Even had he not heard Azazel scream its name, he would have known it. Inside each person lives that which instinctively knows and recognizes the eternal. This had no more resemblance to the caricatures of angels perpetrated on human art than the epitome of perfection in beauty had with a pile of dung. Unbounded by form, it retained an Identity. It was undeniably a Being, but a Being of such a nature as was almost impossible to comprehend as separate from the eternal fabric of reality.

Tripp shook his head. Though the image and memory remained, the understanding continued to elude him. The encounter had been so short, so unexpected. If only he had been given time to prepare, maybe then he could have better grasped the truth of what he saw. Maybe he wouldn't have blacked out, overwhelmed. Maybe...

Then again, maybe he should be thankful the vision was so brief. Its revelation had banished a Minion into oblivion. What might it have done to him, a mere mortal?

Then his misgivings, which always came when he thought of the Seraph, were just as quickly displaced with a grim determination to once more feel that presence, to revel in its joy and terror. No matter what it took, no matter the cost.

Even his own life.

* * *

Malthusan watched the women talking. Rather, he watched Jaelon. Meeker was pleasant enough on the eyes, but her too-blonde hair cut too short and her too-thin figure made her look like a prepubescent boy. Jaelon, on the other hand, was a fine figure of a woman.

Once, long ago, when he was a different person, he might have treated her differently. Before his own Vision, he had been a mercenary, a worshiper of gold with shifting allegiances and little conscience. In these days, his type would be called a soldier of fortune, a genteel term to describe men who hired out their killing instinct to the highest bidder. Murderers for sale, violent men whose fate had landed their vicious spirits in the hands of men with like mind but lesser courage. In that world, men were the enemy and women were spoils of the victor, to be taken as prize along with the rest of the livestock.

Why he had been chosen out of all his fellows to be given the Vision was a question he seldom considered. His vocation rarely required independent thought. He followed orders, and that was enough. He considered that the Vision simply changed his commander to a permanent rather than a temporary one. The deeper philosophical reasons didn't interest him, although once in a while, like now, he wondered what might have brought him to the Master's attention as being worthy.

Jaelon was pacing the porch now. Malthusan found himself admiring her carriage, the grace of her stride. What a contrast to his own deliberate step, his own martial foot.

"She is beautiful, is she not, in her own way?"

Malthusan didn't rise to Populus' words.

"Someday you might tell her so," the other went on.

Malthusan refused to acknowledge the Greek's jibe. It was an old game they played which started the day Populus realized Malthusan had feelings, contrary to his reputation as a cold-blooded killer. Populus probably thought he was walking the edge but Malthusan found the game oddly amusing. Both men knew Populus was no physical match. He was the sparrow to Malthusan's hawk but like those two, the hawk tolerated the sparrow as an annoyance, a silent testimony to his lethality.

"I think Mason may be attracted to her," Populus said.

Malthusan grunted his derision of that statement.

"No, really. And Jaelon may feel the same way. Did you see how she protected him from Azazel?"

"That is why we are here," Malthusan reminded him. "To protect and aid them all."

"Still, she was very quick to step between them," Populus went on. "You were closer."

Malthusan looked sharply at the Greek then. "What do you mean by that?"

Populus shrugged. "Just that Jaelon was quicker. Or perhaps had more reason to come to his aid."

A growl rose in Malthusan's throat. "Do not question my loyalty to the mission, Greek."

The smaller man held up his hands in surrender. "I am not, believe me. I know you are faithful. It is just, where Jaelon is concerned I am sometimes unclear as to your attitude."

"Mind your *own* attitude," Malthusan snapped.

Perhaps sensing the game had stretched a bit too far, Populus nodded. "So I will," he said, moving off a few steps. "Nevertheless, maybe it is time she knew."

Malthusan glared at his retreating back. Sometimes the Greek could be more than an annoyance but in Malthusan's heart he knew the little man was usually right about most everything.

He looked at Jaelon again, talking with Meeker, and was surprised to feel a twisting in his chest.

* * *

Populus left Malthusan brooding and went to see how Martin was doing. The computer expert was putting up a brave front but Populus could see the man was still in pain from the injuries he got when his house was burned. Azazel, or one of his lackeys, had beaten him badly, breaking both his legs, setting the house afire, and leaving him for dead. Martin had managed to crawl from the burning ruins and collapse in the roadway. Smoke rising from the conflagration alerted his neighbors, who arrived in time to save him. Another hour or so would have been too late.

He most identified with Martin. Jaelon and Malthusan weren't given to the attraction to technology he had. Long fascinated with mechanical things, Populus had easily adapted to the computer-controlled present. To him, computers were the ultimate servants: intelligent, obedient, inerrant. From the earliest adding machines to the modern full-immersion interface, Populus made it his personal challenge to be master of the machine. He even tinkered and experimented on his own with new designs. Meeting Martin made him want to putter again with the thinking machines.

He found Martin mumbling to himself over some data displayed on his PDA. The man seemed intensely preoccupied, so Populus waited patiently, watching. Martin jabbed at the PDA in irritation, still mumbling. The machine beeped plaintively. Martin sighed. He noticed Populus standing nearby.

"Hello," Martin said, fingers poised over the PDA as if ready to strike. "Something?"

"Can I help? I have some expertise at mathematics and computers."

Martin eyed him for a moment, then looked back at the PDA. "Maybe," he said. "I've been trying to build a security code to protect our new server."

"New server?"

"Yeah. When we found out that Azazel cracked our security, we asked the South African cell to work up a system based on the diamond trade industry's security. What they came up with is good, but when I tested it I broke through way too easily. Army equipment is just so advanced over commercial software it walks all over their security. Mason agrees with me. What we really need is something equal to our own cracking software. I don't want this Andrael character pulling off something like Azazel did."

Populus nodded. "I understand. I assume you started by identifying your system weaknesses?"

"Yes. There aren't many, but what there are, are serious." Martin clucked his tongue and shook his head. "Army security is outdated, Populus. We should have seen this coming long ago."

"Your system worked well. We seldom see a need to improve on something unless we actually see a flaw. Recriminations are useless. Learn and move on." Populus leaned over the PDA. "Now, what do we have to work with?"

* * *

Mason could hear Populus and Martin in the office bantering computer speak. Through the front windows he saw Jaelon and Meeker deep in conversation, Malthusan leaning against a porch column watching. Clattering from the kitchen told him Overguard was making dinner. Tripp sat staring into his water glass, making odd noises.

He was worried about Tripp. The man had not spoken a dozen words since they got back. What few responses he had given were monosyllabic and distracted. Mason was not used to Tripp being so introspective. The man's normal joviality was muted, nearly to the point you could call him morose.

Overguard came to the kitchen door. "Dinner in twenty," he announced, wiping his hands on a towel. "Lasagna tonight."

"Sounds great," Mason replied.

Tripp didn't look as if he heard. Mason walked toward the kitchen, signaling Overguard to follow.

"What's up?" Overguard asked when they got into the kitchen.

Mason leaned against the countertop. "Have you noticed how distracted Tripp is?"

"I figured he was just shook up a little more than the rest of us," Overguard said. He walked to a cabinet and started pulling out plates.

"No, I think it's more than that," Mason said.

"What do you mean?"

"I don't know exactly. It's like he's in another world altogether. I've never seen him like this before."

Overguard frowned. "Is that bad? I always thought he was kinda off, anyway. Frankly, not having him being 'his normal self' is a blessing."

Mason glowered at him. "Be nice."

The big man shrugged and checked the oven.

"You say he left the van to help me?"

"Yeah, just a couple minutes before you sent us to check on Martin."

"That would have been..." Mason stopped. The series of events flashed through his mind. Azazel's attack, the Knights' defense, the ultimatum, the Minion's refusal, the Knights' attack, then their suggestion to send the others away.

Of course! The Knights sent the others away because no one but him was supposed to see the climax of that battle. It must have been their plan that he was the only one to see the Seraph, but Tripp hadn't stuck to the plan.

Tripp must have seen it, but how much of it did he see? What Mason saw had been mitigated, he was sure, by the Knights' presence. What Azazel saw finished him off. What

Tripp saw must have been somewhere between, a harrowing thought. Mason's own experience still burned bright in his mind.

"You look like you've seen a ghost," Overguard observed.

Mason ignored him and went back into the front room. Tripp hadn't moved. Mason walked around in front of him and knelt to get eye level with his seated friend.

"John."

Tripp didn't seem to hear.

"You saw it, didn't you?" Mason put his hand on Tripp's arm. "You saw the Seraph."

His pronunciation of the word stirred something in Tripp. The man's head came up, though his eyes remained unfocused, as if he saw nothing.

"John, talk to me. Did you see it?"

Tripp gave off a long sigh, almost a groan and his eyes closed slowly. "So...beautiful," he breathed, almost inaudibly.

"My God," Overguard said from the kitchen door. "He actually saw it?"

"If he had, he'd be dead," Mason said, still looking for signs of lucidity in Tripp's face. "Like me, he probably only got a glimpse."

"And it did *that* to him?"

Mason didn't answer. He shook Tripp's arm. "John, you have to snap out of it. Open your eyes and look at me."

Tripp's eyes popped open, and for just a second Mason thought he saw an image there, the reflection of that Being that burned Azazel into oblivion by its very presence. Nearly as quickly, though, it was gone and Tripp's eyes focused on him. Mason could almost see the sanity pouring back into that gaze from its hiding place it went to escape that image.

"Mason?" Tripp said. He looked around. "What's wrong?"

"Are you all right?" Mason asked.

Tripp blinked several times and nodded. "Sure. Sorry. I guess I nodded off." He looked at the other two. "Was I having a nightmare or something?"

Mason stood up. "Something like that."

"Well, I'm okay. Really," Tripp assured them. "Thanks."

A pregnant silence settled over the room.

"I really am okay," Tripp insisted.

Overguard looked at Mason, then went back into the kitchen. Mason settled into the high-backed chair across from Tripp. He crossed his legs and tapped his chin with a forefinger.

"John, may I ask you something?"

"Of course," Tripp said.

"How much did you see at the park? Really?"

Tripp shifted in his seat and cleared his throat. Mason could tell the man was thinking about his answer. Trying to figure a way to lie about it? Or just trying to find the words?

"You saw the Seraph, didn't you?" Mason blurted before Tripp could answer.

Tripp looked stunned for a moment. He shifted again. "I... uh..."

Mason waited. Eventually Tripp would have to admit the truth or make some kind of excuse, but he wasn't going to let the man get away with not answering the question.

"Yes," Tripp said at last, sighing. "Yes, I saw it."

"You want to talk about it?"

Tripp tilted his head at Mason. "What?"

"About how it felt. How you feel now about what you saw."

"I don't know what you mean."

Mason uncrossed his legs and leaned forward. "Come on, John, you've been like a zombie since we got back. Talk to me."

"There's nothing to talk about," Tripp said with a shrug.

Mason stared at his friend, watched as Tripp turned his

face away and twirled his glass nervously in his hands. There was obviously no reason to go on asking him about it. They had been together far too long for Mason not to know when Tripp was dead-set against something, and it was obvious this was one of those things. Mason tried to imagine what it must be like to try and contain the feelings that had wracked him so deeply. The memory of the sight of the Seraph still sent shivers up his spine and echoes of that emotional tidal wave sounded in the back of his mind. Just a glimpse from behind the protection of the Knights.

He just hoped that whatever Tripp was holding inside wouldn't turn against them.

* * *

Overguard left Mason talking with Tripp and worked on finishing dinner. He admitted he wasn't the best cook in their troop, but he volunteered to do it sometimes, and no one yet had complained. He might not make the best coffee, but he had great pride in his Italian, especially his lasagna. Janice kidded him about it. He let her, but nobody else was allowed.

The smell of the dish cooking always reminded him of happier times when he was little, long before The Army had entered his life. Long before Mexico.

Here it was, all these years later, and he still got a bitter taste in his mouth. Survivor guilt, it was called. It wasn't his fault he hadn't been there when The Enemy raided his cell and killed everyone. He was away on assignment, doing his duty. He had no reason to feel guilty, and yet he did.

Still, the Master must have had a hand in it all somehow. If he hadn't left Mexico, he would have never have been assigned to Mason's cell, never met Janice in that coffee house in Amsterdam, never found what little peace he now had. Janice was a balm on his pain, a blessing he never failed to appreciate.

Men in The Army usually avoided romantic entanglements. It hurt too much to see the ones you spent emotional currency on age and die while you remained young and vibrant. He'd done that only once before, and sometimes he could still see the bewilderment in her eyes as she came to realize the difference between them. How do you explain to someone you love that they will most assuredly move on while you remain? It must be like how the doctor feels when telling a patient they have a terminal illness. Kind of a detached sadness; a sympathetic, vicarious, fearful pain.

He didn't have to worry about that with Janice. She would stay with him until the end. It was a great comfort to know that. So many people had gone away, through no fault of their own. Taken by death through accident or sickness or murder, they had gone on to the reward that awaited all, a reward delayed but not eliminated for him.

He checked the timer. Still long enough to make the salad before popping the bread into the oven. He pulled out the makings and set about his task.

It was odd to think that until recently none of them had actually met in person. Until the incident with Azazel, they had only ever got together in the computer-generated virtual city of E-Yukon, in a small farm house just outside the city limits. He had liked that old place. It reminded him a lot of home, of his younger days. He grew up on a farm not unlike that simulacrum. One hundred and twenty acres of farm and grazing land set in the plains states. Cattle and corn and wheat and rye. A quiet existence. How could he have ever thought it boring? How could he have ever wanted to leave?

Yes, it was the stupid restlessness of youth that eventually drove him from those idyllic surroundings into the bustling streets of Las Vegas. And it was those streets that stripped away any idealistic vision he had of the outside world. When you have no money and don't speak the local lingo, it's easy to quickly find yourself on the wrong side of town, and he did. He never found out what it was TheArmy recruiter saw about him, but he was grateful to be pulled out of that hell hole, even if it was to become part of a never-ending Conflict.

He sighed. The past was the past. There was no going back to change what had been. All he could do was look to the future and hope to make it better, for himself and Janice. Never again would he find himself a sole survivor. Never again would he be separated from his companions.

The oven alarmed beeped. Time to brown the bread.

*　*　*

The office screamed wealth. The walls were hung with masterpieces from the far ends of the world. Furniture made from the rarest woods graced its ornately carved marble floor. Artifacts older than most civilizations stood in proud displays strategically located between the paintings. The man behind the office desk was just as impeccably accoutered and well-groomed. The room conveyed a quiet dignity and grace the man did not feel.

"This is unacceptable!"

Andrew Nicholson, CFO of Catalina Industries and known to his operatives as Andrael, glowered at the face in the visiplate. The device was embedded in a panel that rose from his desk at the touch of a button. He leaned against that desk, where the computer built into its surface displayed information confirming his subordinate's report. The opulence of his surroundings did little to assuage his anger.

"How is it possible they could just disappear?" he said, frustrated. He had the databases, surveillance equipment, and intelligence capabilities of Catalina Industries and, through the parent corporation Andlat Enterprises, the information from nearly every country on the planet to draw upon. It was incredible. For all intents and purposes, Azazel's killers had vanished. They must have a significant organization behind them to be able to come and go so readily without being detected.

Nicholson ground his teeth together. He needed those files. Without them, he couldn't get to the server back door, and every day those people had the files was another chance they had to discover the secret. If they were able to hide from his intelligence system, they were capable of cracking the security on those files.

"I want them found and dealt with now!" he commanded the lackey. "Start at Jenkins'. Run his security tapes and follow up with facial recognition software."

"But sir, if Andlat can't find them, how can..."

"Just do it!" he shouted. He jabbed at the controls to cut off the connection. "Moron!" He shook himself and took a deep breath. "I'm surrounded by idiots!" With an effort, he calmed himself. He lowered the visiplate into its place and sat down at the desk to think.

It was obvious that if he was going to find these people, he would probably have to do it himself. He couldn't afford to trust anyone else in Catalina without the possibility Azrael would find out. He hated having to get his hands dirty, but without Azazel he didn't have much choice.

He hit the intercom. "Jessie."

"Yes, Mr. Nicholson?" came the voice of his personal assistant.

"Cancel everything for the next week."

3

Someone once said an army runs on its stomach, and theirs was no exception. The addition of the Knights put an unexpected strain on Mason's pantry, so they soon found it necessary to reprovision. After some argument, Mason gave in to Jaelon's insistence they go along.

The Knights' van could seat eight and still had room for an impressive arsenal of non-lethal weaponry neatly organized against its internal walls. The windshield and side windows were heavily tinted to dissuade the curious. From outside it looked like a nondescript black panel van. Inside it was a full-blown battle wagon, heavily armed and well-equipped.

Overguard discovered Jaelon's weapon of choice was an odd contraption she called a mace but held little resemblance to the medieval weapon. Although he knew it wasn't designed to kill, it certainly looked lethal enough to intimidate any opponent.

Malthusan carried no visible weapons. Not that it mattered. The man's fists were big enough to stand for clubs.

As for Populus, well, Overguard didn't think the man was really built for physical combat. He had been surprised when Populus left with the other two to face Azazel. There was obviously more to that man than met the eye.

The trip into Memphis took about an hour, time Tripp spent in complete silence. Overguard glanced at him occasionally, not quite sure what to make of the man's quiet. The three Knights rode in the rear of the van while Mason drove and Meeker rode shotgun.

The four lane highway compressed to two as they approached the Memphis suburbs. Mason swung the van into the parking area of the first store they encountered. Several people fueling their vehicles looked up at the van as it rolled to a stop away from the smaller parking slots, but no one showed more than a passing interest. Several other vans and some larger trucks were parked nearby. The Knights' van looked like just another commercial vehicle to them.

Mason turned in his seat. "Who's going in?"

Jaelon looked at Malthusan. The big man nodded and opened the panel to step aside.

A harsh metallic ping sounded and Malthusan jumped back. Three more sharp thunks followed as the panel slid to. Malthusan sat back down and looked at Jaelon.

"Somebody is shooting at us," he observed.

Overguard pushed forward and motioned Meeker toward the back. She slipped around him as he settled into the passenger seat. He and Mason peered through the driver side window. Two slaps sounded against the bulletproof glass, exactly where Mason's eyes showed. The bullets didn't penetrate, but the van rocked gently.

"Seems so," Mason agreed. He started the van. "Hold on to something."

The other people in the parking lot were looking around in confusion. The shooter was using a silencer, but the sound of the rounds ricocheting off the van was far from quiet. They knew something out of the ordinary was happening, but the true nature of the danger hadn't dawned on them yet. It wasn't until Mason yanked on the wheel and the big van roared out of the parking lot that some of them began running. The van bounced onto the road with a heavy rattle. Overguard craned his neck to check the rear view display built into the dashboard. Three cars pulled out in pursuit. Meeker was standing at the rear now, looking out the back windows.

"Two men in the front car, one in the second," she announced. "I can see weapons in the first one. Can't tell about the other."

Overguard caught a series of flashes in the display coming from the front car. The staccato bangs of multiple rounds hitting the van testified to an automatic weapon.

"Get on the interstate," they heard Populus say.

Mason yanked the van into a bank that threatened to lift the right hand tires off the ground to catch the entry ramp they almost passed. Overguard felt a tap on his shoulder.

"Excuse me, old man," Populus said. "May I?"

Overguard relinquished his seat and the Greek dropped into it.

"Where am I going?" Mason asked.

Populus waved ahead. "Just drive."

* * *

Mason floored the van as they reached the interstate lanes. The vehicle all but leaped forward. He inwardly cursed the government for not keeping the interstate in better condition as he struggled to negotiate it. He could hear activity in the van behind him, but didn't dare turn to look. The digital speedometer was going through 130 KPH and rising. He wasn't sure the vehicle was made for high speed. Its box-like shape didn't promise much.

Populus was rummaging through a compartment he had somehow opened in the dashboard in front of him. Mason chanced a look and caught the man slipping on an interface headset. The Greek reached into the compartment and fiddled with something there.

"Take the second exit," Populus said. "I'll see what I can do."

Mason had no idea what the man meant, but this was no time to ask questions. There were too many cracks and holes in the pavement to avoid. Another spate of bullet impacts told him their pursuers were still there.

"Second car coming around," Meeker announced tensely. "I was wrong. There are two men in it as well. Looks like he's..." There was a series of metallic pings and slaps. "Yep. He's armed, too."

Mason saw the exit coming and waited until the last second before yanking the steering wheel right. The right side wheels did come off the ground that time. He heard someone in the back crash into the side of the van.

"Watch it!" Overguard shouted at him.

"Sorry," Mason said, struggling to put the van back on four wheels again. A glance at the rear view display told him one of the cars made the turn. The other, the one that was trying to come alongside, missed it. Its driver made the mistake of trying to jump the slope and follow. The car flew off the rise and spun lazily in the air before coming down on its roof and bursting into flame. Its companion narrowly missed hitting the wreck, then sped after the van.

"That was stupid," Mason heard Meeker observe.

One down, two to go.

Mason slowed the van as they approached the end of the exit ramp. Traffic on the road ahead meant new problems.

"Don't slow down!" Populus snapped.

As if in response to his command, the car become heavier and seem to crouch closer to the road. Mason slammed the accelerator open again. The van jumped forward. Mason grit his teeth as he leaned into the curve at the end of the ramp to join the main road. Surprisingly, the vehicle clung tenaciously to the pavement. It took just a moment for him to realize this was no accident. He chuckled to himself at the thought, then he abandoned any concern they might flip the van and hit the accelerator to its stops. The van had become surprisingly nimble for its size. Mason heard Overguard grumbling in the back as he weaved back and forth through the traffic.

"Take the second left," Populus said.

Mason didn't even flinch as they crossed two lanes of traffic and turned against the light. There was a series of crashes behind them. In the rear view he saw their pursuer's car sideswipe another and launch into the air over the curb to disappear into a ball of flame against the opposite side of the intersection. Cars careened like ants scattering away from the fire.

"Third car's breaking off," Meeker announced. "Looks like they've had enough."

Mason didn't let up on the accelerator. "For now," he thought.

* * *

Nicholson cursed under his breath as he watched the cars burn. The satellite surveillance of the pursuit told him the whole story, except who the hell were these people? Not even his best men could bring them in? He was absolutely convinced now that they weren't free agents. Somebody was behind them, somebody with serious resources. There was no other explanation. But who?

There had to be a way to get to them. Nothing was impossible. That was his personal motto. He had it imprinted on a plaque that hung on the wall across from his desk as a constant reminder. It had served him well in his rise through the ranks of Catalina Industries. From his first job as a personal assistant to his position now of CFO, he had refused to take 'no' for an answer. When his co-workers said it couldn't be done, he found a way. Beg, borrow, or steal, he'd found a way. He always made sure to keep a little back, just enough to always have an edge. As a result, he was both admired and feared by his peers. He made sure the balance sheet in all transactions left him in the black and his opponents in the red.

Andrew Nicholson was not accustomed to losing, yet here he was on the wrong end of this because the one man he thought could handle the situation had failed him spectacularly.

Damn Jenkins anyway! All he had to do was misplace

some files. How tough was that? A simple computer glitch would do it, and it looked as if it worked. The Catalina Industries files in Panama got hit by what the IT guys called an internet virus. Nicholson had smiled at the news. Brilliant, he thought. An impersonal attack on a corporate server? How better to disguise the job? He had been ready to go the next stage in his plan when Jenkins called with his demands.

Fool! Try to blackmail him? If the other group hadn't done it, Nicholson would have seen to Jenkins himself. They had done him a favor there, but that left the disturbing question unanswered of who they were and how much they knew.

He hated loose ends.

* * *

Back at Mason's house, Martin pulled off the modified I/O and whooped victoriously.

"Got you, you rotten bastard!" he shouted, pointing at the screen. He turned to look around, then realized no one was home to share his celebration. "Typical," he groused to the computer. "Never around when you need 'em."

The front door burst open. Wards went off, sending shock waves through the house. The aroma of roses washed past him. Something yelped in pain. Furniture crashed.

"Not again," Martin breathed. He hit the off button on his laptop. He pulled the USB drive free. "Why me?" he whispered to himself. Moving as quickly as he dared, he rolled back away from the computer and opened the rear door of the room. It fed into the master bedroom. He tossed the USB drive under the bed and quietly closed the door.

He was rolling back to the office door when the men came in, weapons lowered at him.

"Hi guys," he grinned at them. "Can I get you something to drink?"

* * *

"If they were this close to the safe house, it's past time to move our base," Jaelon observed.

The van sped down the two-lane blacktop toward Mason's house. Something nibbled around the edge of Mason's consciousness, an uneasy feeling. He pressed on the accelerator, but it was already down full.

"What's wrong?" Populus asked from his position in the passenger seat.

Mason didn't answer. He was busy negotiating the last

curve before his white gravel drive came into view.

Two black SUVs sat blocking the road. The armed men standing beside them opened fire on the Knights' van.

Mason yanked the wheel hard left, presenting the side of the van to the enemy. The van slid hard into the SUVs, scattering the shooters and knocking the SUVs off the road into the ditches either side. The enemy kept up a constant fusillade as Mason backed the van into one SUV and whirled back onto the road. He made the turn onto the gravel with a few inches to spare on his side from the iron gate, spraying rocks.

They thundered down the drive to find the house was under attack, not that you would have known it had you not been initiated into the kind of attack. From the outside, the place looked normal except that the front door stood wide open.

Mason hoped Martin was still alive.

The van careened to a stop and everyone piled out. Running low, they sprinted for the back door of the house. Bullets ricocheted off the brick and broke windows as they ran. Mason shouted the wards off as they vaulted the deck railing and slammed into the door.

He brought up short at the overpowering stench of rot, pushing down nausea. The origin of the stink was wallowing in pain, pinned to the floor by the wards Mason set before leaving.

It looked vaguely like a dog, if a dog had two heads melted into one, an appropriate number of teeth, and was the size of a small horse. As they watched, it broke the first ward and staggered to its feet. It howled as it bounced off the boundary runes and paced back and forth, snuffling. Jaelon and Malthusan pushed him to the side as the thing turned to face them.

"I don't think that ward is going to hold it long," Populus said from the doorway.

"Find Martin!" Mason yelled at Overguard.

Overguard worked his way around the scene to dive through a side door and disappear.

The beast leapt at them and rebounded with a yelp of rage.

"What is it?" Meeker's eyes were round with fear.

"Some kind of *scucca*," Jaelon said, motioning her in and to the side.

"What?"

"It's a demon," Malthusan said, and moved to stand between her and the thing. "That's all you need to know."

"What are we going to do?" she asked, voice shaking.

"You're not going to do anything," Malthusan barked. "Except stop talking."

Populus moved to stand beside Jaelon. He exchanged a

look with her and Malthusan. As one, they extended their arms to their sides. The air between them rippled. The beast stopped and watched them warily. It tried to back up, but the ward held it in the room.

The ripple floated away from the Knights and across the room, through the ward as if it wasn't there. The demon whined and tried to make itself smaller against the far side of the ward. The ripple touched it and it howled in agony. Mason watched in horrified fascination as its skin bubbled and blistered. It writhed and twisted sinuously until the body crumpled into a blackened mass that smoked heavily for several seconds before falling into a putrescent stain.

With its disappearance, the ward and the ripple both vanished as well. The Knights dropped their arms.

"Odd," Populus said, looking at the stain. "Why send such a minor threat?"

"It was a message," Jaelon said.

"I'm more worried about the men outside," Malthusan said, striding toward the front door.

Overguard appeared from the office door. "No need. They're gone. That demon wasn't a message. It was a diversion. They took Martin."

They piled into the office and sifted through the debris.

There had been a struggle. Martin might have been in a wheelchair, but he hadn't gone quietly.

The computer was a mess. Whoever took Martin must have used the butt of a large weapon on it. Mason grunted in frustration at the sight of the mutilated machine.

"Well, we're not using that anymore," Populus said. He looked around the room. "They must have taken his laptop as well."

"Computers can be replaced," Mason growled. "We need to find Martin." Inwardly, he cursed himself. If he had taken the proper precautions and moved them after Azrael had found his home, this would never have happened. Once again he had needlessly placed his cell in danger and now they had lost a valued member and personal friend. When would he learn?

"I guess Andrael has what he wanted now," Meeker supposed, sadly. "The USB drive is gone. Martin is the only one who knows how to use it, anyway. All of our bargaining chips are gone."

"My dear Janice," Populus inserted. "You forget Mr. Martin and I were working together on this. All is not lost."

"Besides that," Jaelon said, "the summoning of the *scucca* gives us some information as well."

"What kind of information?" Meeker asked.

"We know that whoever this Andrael is, he or someone in his employ can summon. That means we're dealing with another Minion."

Meeker tossed her head and rolled her eyes. "Wonderful! Like we didn't have enough to worry about."

"This is getting complicated," Overguard groused. "Did Andrael take Martin or was it Azrael? Who do we track to get him back? If it was Andrael that took him, then Azrael is still looking for the files and we can't let him know we lost them. If it was Azrael that took Martin, then Andrael doesn't know and he'll still be after us. In that case, Azrael will probably just write us off completely, let Andrael do what he can to take us out."

"Huh?" Meeker said.

"I doubt Azrael took Martin," Populus said. "Why would he? If he had the files, all he would be interested in would be destroying them. We know he doesn't care that much about Mason's cell. He sees Mason more as an ally than an enemy. Andrael, on the other hand, would want to know how much we had gleaned from the drive. It's a fair bet that Martin is still alive if only for that reason."

"One thing's for sure," Tripp put in. "We can't stay here."

"No, we can't," Mason agreed. "Everybody pack up. We move out in an hour."

"Where to?" Overguard asked.

"West."

* * *

It was Overguard who found the USB drive under the bed during the packing sweep. The discovery lifted their spirits a bit. At least that much was still in their possession. Unfortunately, it meant Martin was likely to be questioned vigorously by his captors. The man was barely recovered from his injuries. Mason wasn't sure how long Martin might last under interrogation. He didn't think Martin would betray them, even under extreme circumstances, but he hated to think his friend was going through something like that because they hadn't been there to protect him.

The computers in the Knights' van had been adapted to the improved I/O devices as soon as Martin and Populus designed them, so it took only a matter of minutes to get the devices plugged in. Luckily, Martin's abductors didn't know what the interface headsets were. Outwardly they were no different than any commercially available interface, so they probably thought it wasn't worth their effort to destroy them. Populus ran diagnostics on each anyway, just in case, before putting them into service.

They decided to explore the Catalina Industries files on the chance something in the Catalina Industries servers might give them a clue as to Martin's whereabouts. Meeker volunteered to jack in while the rest of the crew packed the van and searched the house for anything they might have missed.

Populus handed Meeker the I/O set. He smiled at her as she donned the device and nodded.

"Ready," Populus said, hand poised over the control panel.

"Yes," Meeker affirmed.

"Three. Two. One."

* * *

It was raining. Lightning flashed in the distance and the wind whipped the rain into her facing, stinging her skin. Meeker was always astonished at how complete the VR environment became when she wore Martin's I/Os. It was such a difference from the regular ones.

"How are you?"

She spun to find a robed man standing just behind her. The avatar was the spitting image of Populus, right down to the hair and eye color.

"Good," she told him. She looked around. Nothing was shaped correctly, and all the colors of the landscape were shifting peculiarly. She felt her stomach lurch, watching.

"Concentrate on the glyphs," Populus suggested. "Don't spend too much time sightseeing. The disorientation will eject you from the connection. A security precaution, I guess."

"Okay." She looked at the angelic script hanging in midair before her. "Which one is Andrael?"

Populus reached out and double-tapped a sigil. The others disappeared and a new set became visible. Populus pointed at one.

"Azazel," he read. He scanned the others. "These others are all human names transcribed. There seems to be a suffix on each. Could denote rank, or importance."

"Which one would be most important?"

Populus paused, then pointed at one near the end of the line. "That one would be my guess. It has the most characters in its suffix."

"What's the name?"

"Andrew Nicholson."

"Then that's the one we'll try."

Populus nodded. "I'll hold the connection open. Once you're in, find the server IP. The VR should render it as a signpost or something similar. Memorize it and punch out. Got it?"

Meeker nodded.

"You shouldn't run into any problems. We're pretty far past the system security. If you do, though, the VR will identify it and present it in the form of a threat. Avoid any entanglements, or you'll set off the system alerts."

"Got it," she said. "How do I punch out?"

Populus laughed. "Sorry. Here." He held out his hand. A small vial appeared and he handed it to her. "That's your out. Drink it or throw it on the ground and break it. Either way will jack you out instantly. If you lose it somehow, visualize the I/O around your neck. The VR should manifest it for you to manually remove."

"Okay."

"Good luck," the Knight said.

"Thanks." She reached out and double-tapped the Nicholson sigil.

She was transported into a large modern office. It was sparsely furnished, nothing more than a couple of hard backed chairs, a large desk, and its seat. The walls were blank except for a single certificate behind the desk. It bore several numbers and nothing else. She assumed that was the IP.

"Identify," a voice from behind her said.

She twirled. She found herself confronted with a humanoid figure. It was uniformly gray, sexless, and wore nothing except what looked like a digital stopwatch in its hand. The digital watch pinged.

"Identification failed. Identify," it demanded.

She was confused. What did it want? It didn't appear to be a threat. Still, if she didn't identify herself as authorized to be there, what then? Populus had said to avoid confrontations. She fingered the little vial nervously.

The digital watch pinged.

"Identification failed. Identify," it repeated.

A password! That's what it wanted. And didn't systems kick you out if you failed to give the right password three times in a row? This was its third request. It was getting ready to log her off if she didn't come up with something quick.

"Andrael!" she blurted, then a sick thrill went through her. Why had she said that? What if it was wrong? She got ready to throw the vial.

"Identification accepted."

It ceased to exist. Meeker sighed in relief.

Then she gasped. The office was no longer empty. Gorgeous paintings hung from the walls. The furniture had become plush and expensive pieces, while the desk was changed into an incredible piece of technology. She couldn't resist looking at its surface, covered in computer displays and controls.

"I wish Populus was here," she muttered, scanning the multi-colored keys.

"Do you think he would know how to use that panel any better than you?"

Meeker jumped. The avatar had appeared out of nowhere. It was the shape of a man, a little better than average height, well-dressed. The details were minimal, as though the VR was trying to put together a profile from very little information.

"Hello." He smiled at her. "I'm Andrew Nicholson. And you are?"

She threw the vial.

She blinked at the sudden change. Populus sat across from her in the van, still inside the simulation. She had to get back in to let him know what had happened, but suddenly realized she didn't really know how. Panic rose in her chest.

Populus cleared his throat and removed the I/O device. "So, did you get the IP?" he asked.

She almost cried out in relief. The Knight put out his hand to steady her.

"What's wrong?" He pulled her I/O device off her neck and hit the controls to deactivate it.

"Nicholson came online while I was there," she said. "He knew I was there."

Populus frowned. "What did he say?"

"He told me his name and asked who I was."

"Did you tell him?"

She scoffed. "Of course not!"

The Knight nodded thoughtfully. "No disrespect meant, my dear. Sometimes our avatar's artificial intelligence responds to identity queries automatically without our permission."

"Oh," she said, mollified.

"Can you describe his avatar?"

"There wasn't much to it. Just a man in a business suit," she replied.

"Understandable," Populus said. "The VR didn't have a lot to work with. What information it might have was only available from the computer you accessed, which probably only had the minimum necessary about the operator. Passwords, gender, age, that kind of thing." He got up. "Do you remember the IP address?"

She sighed. "I'm sorry. Only a couple of the numbers, not the whole thing."

"Well, it can't be helped then. We'll have to go back in some other way. I need to let Mason and the others know about this."

"Did we just hurt Martin?" she worried.

Populus stopped. "I sincerely hope not, my dear."

4

Nicholson scowled. The hack was very professionally done. If he hadn't logged in at just that moment, he would never have known about it. The female avatar resembled the face of one of the people who had been in the group that killed Jenkins. Somehow, that group had cracked his security codes and accessed his files. How far into his system they'd reached was anybody's guess.

Who *were* these people? It wasn't the first time he'd asked that question. He fumed at the inefficiency of his own personnel compared to this troop of assassins. They'd foiled him at every turn, seemingly effortlessly. The possibility they were working for Azrael was more likely with each encounter. How else could they know how to get into his computers? How else could they know so much about his organization? They must have taken the files off Jenkins, the ones Jenkins threatened to use against him. They were using those files not only to protect Azrael, but to destroy him.

He flirted with the idea of just picking up and disappearing. Would that it were that easy. He knew better. There was no place to go that Azrael couldn't find him. He was committed. He had to see this through to the end, or very likely would die trying. He had to move forward, get out ahead of this again.

He put his IT crew on tracing the hack. They worked only a few hours before reporting back to him that after a thorough check they could find no evidence of a security breach.

Whoever that woman was, she had better people working with her.

He sat at his desk, fuming. He knew what he saw. He knew there had been a breach, and he was convinced it was connected with Jenkins' death. Had Dorian Azrael hired her? What was she really doing? He went over his files again, running his own diagnostics on every one. He didn't really expect to find anything. His own computer expertise didn't compare to his IT lackeys'. He just felt the need to do something, anything, than take the word of someone else that it hadn't happened when he knew it had.

Finally, he sat back and sighed. As expected, he had

found nothing. No keyloggers, no worms, no viruses, no trojans, no bots, no rootkits, no malware, not a single unauthorized payload of any kind.

So, why was he still nervous?

If she didn't leave anything behind, then she must have been looking for something. What had she learned, and why? He needed to find her and get that from her. No matter what it took.

The first step was to identify her, but the only thing he had to go by so far was the avatar. Maybe that would be enough.

"Avatar build," he commanded.

The computer generated a blank humanoid. Faceless, featureless, nothing but a mannikin.

"Female. Short blond hair. Slight build. Five feet six inches tall."

Slowly, the computer adjusted the avatar to his description. He eyed it critically. The face was still a blank.

"Light complexion. Medium features."

A face coalesced, but there wasn't enough resolution.

"Zoom to face."

The body disappeared as the mannikin's visage expanded until it took up most of his field of vision.

"Round the eyes plus ten percent. Eye color green.

No, hazel. Mouth broader. Not that broad. Cheeks not as full. Chin sharper. More. Stop. Nose thinner. More. Stop. Eyebrows thinner. Stop."

He nodded. That was her. At least, that was her avatar.

"Process and identify," he commanded.

The small delay while the computer complied with his directive seemed hours, but was only a few seconds. The picture of a woman replaced the avatar, but it was evident this was the woman on which the avatar must have been designed.

"Janice Meeker," the computer AI announced. "Born Cedar Rapids, Iowa, United States. Emigrated to Netherlands, European Block. Graduated University of Amsterdam. Employed as personal assistant to local accountancy firm. Disappeared three years ago. Whereabouts unknown."

"Last known address?" he asked.

"Haäsdanger Boardinghouse, Amsterdam, the Netherlands, European Block."

He smiled. At least he had a place to start.

"Get me Security."

* * *

Harold Martin blinked hard when they removed the hood. In a few seconds his eyes adjusted to the glare of the fluorescent lighting and he quickly took in his surroundings.

Two armed men stood near the metal door to his left, the only exit from the room. A plain rectangular table stood between him and the woman sitting across it. The man who lifted the hood slipped quietly between the guards and left the room without a word. There was no other furniture than the table and his opponent's chair. The walls were a dull gray under a celotex ceiling. He felt like he'd stepped back in time to the last years of the 20th century.

The guards stood looking at nothing though he caught the subtle signs they were ready to respond to any untoward action on is part, holsters loosed and hands by their sides, feet spread apart, waiting.

The woman watched him patiently as he assessed his position. She waited until he looked directly at her to address him in a pleasant bass soprano voice that made him wonder if he'd misidentified her gender. She had dark brown hair that fell in a thick cascade over her shoulders, large eyes as brown as her hair, full lips and high cheekbones. Under other circumstances, he might have considered her attractive, but the steel in her eyes told him there would be nothing but business between them.

That, and the unmistakable scent of lilac.

"I believe you know why you are here," she stated. "So, where is it?"

"What?"

She motioned with her left hand. A previously unseen panel opened in the table.

"I will ask you again." Her voice was unhurried and patient. "Where is it?"

"I don't know what you want," Martin replied.

She tilted her head and looked at him. "Resistance?"

Martin didn't answer. He looked around the room again, then back to her. She sat for a moment as if deliberating her next move, then touched the panel.

He wasn't in the interrogation room any more. The world opened out around him into an alien but familiar landscape. It closely resembled the VR interface he had accessed with the USB files.

"There are things in the human mind, Aaorld Maachen, that should not exist," a disembodied voice echoed across the vista. The pronunciation of his real name, his birth name, the name he'd abandoned so long ago, startled him. How did they know? Hardly anyone living was privy to that secret.

"We know everything about you," the voice said,

responding to his very thoughts. "You cannot hide anything from us here."

They were in his head! They had somehow tapped into his consciousness, the same way the interface devices accessed the brain to allow people to interact with the VR environment of the online game.

"Indeed," said the voice. "So, you see, you can hide nothing from us, for we control your very existence."

They expected him to crumble under this? He laughed.

"Virtual reality is just that," he said to that voice. "You might be able to read my conscious thoughts, but that's really no different than what you can convince me to tell you through drugs or hypnosis." He looked down at himself. He was no longer in the wheelchair. He was clothed in his game avatar. "You've even had to use images you found in the game protocol to place me here. You're in no more control of me and my existence here than you are outside."

A low rumbling began. He listened to it transform into the rhythmic thundering approach of an incredibly large animal. He looked on in astonishment as what could only be a dragon appeared from thin air, roaring and brandishing its membranous wings. Its serpentine body measured a good thirty feet long and when it stood on its hind legs it rose four times his height. Its front legs melded bat-like into the wings, but its neck raised its head half a body length above its shoulders. Great spiked scales covered its back and sides. He was surprised to feel the sound of its roar in his chest, smell the stench of its breath. How complete was this simulation, anyway? The first thrill of fear stung him.

The great animal settled on its haunches and tucked its wings into its sides. Slowly, it lowered its head until it hung even with Martin's. It snorted, blowing Martin's hair back and making his eyes water.

"Mr. Martin, some of what you say is correct. We are not in complete control of your will," the voice admitted. "However, just as your virtual reality simulations are based on *your* reality, did it not occur to you that the simulation within the interface you discovered was also based on reality?"

He could feel the heat coming off the animal, smell its odor so like cloth soaked in sulfur. He stepped carefully backward to gasp for air away from the volume of its breath that encased him roundabout. He could hear its pulse as a great rushing noise against the dirt. The sound of its massive weight shifting as it moved was a combination of scales on metal and an obscene organic sloshing. He gulped back the bile rising in his throat.

The woman appeared between him and the animal, still unperturbed and impassive.

"If you have not already guessed," she told him, "you are in no virtual reality simulation. This," and here she waved expansively to include her surroundings, "is the real world, Mr. Martin. This is where we come from, the true reality, not the pitiful world humans have built from blood and bone and dirt. This is the first creation, the beginning from which all things sprang, including your pitiful ancestors."

Martin swallowed hard. He understood the language of her words, but he wasn't sure he understood their meaning. The true reality? What did that mean? Was this some elaborate trick? To what end?

"You should know, Mr. Martin, that in this world we are the sum total of the law. There are no other influences here. We are the total masters, the only force. There can be no interference with us here, no rescue, no last minute reprieve. You will tell us what we want to know, if we must keep you here forever. We will make you suffer a thousand times more than you have ever suffered before." She tilted her head at him again. "Will you tell us where it is?"

Martin looked at her, then at the beast behind her. He looked around at the landscape that shared nothing with anywhere else he had ever been. He was alone here, without hope of Mason or the Knights finding him. He believed that much of what she'd said. It was obvious he was on his own here. He had been on his own before, but never so isolated from any kind of aid.

He looked into her eyes. There was no mercy there, only patience. They could afford patience, here or elsewhere, because for her kind there never need be urgency about anything. They had eternity to accomplish their goals, and they were perfectly willing to wait that long. The Enemy Minions were of the same cloth as the Master's. Their nature made them obsessive, using every tool and sacrificing anything to gain success in their mission.

He smiled. They might have eternity, but he did not. They knew he only had a relatively little time to give them their answers, no matter how long they might manage to stretch it out. And he had something they didn't.

Certainty. Until that very moment, he hadn't really thought about it. Only now, faced with a near-eternity of pain, did he realize who he was and what he believed. The years of fighting in the Conflict, physically and otherwise, flashed across his mind.

He remembered the train station where he met Mason

in 1915, but most of all he remembered why he'd been there, from what Mason and The Army had rescued him.

The Prussia he was born into was much different than the Germany it became. It was a simple place, with simple people more interested in sowing and harvest and making beer than war. With the impatience and ambition of youth, he abandoned that simple life for travel to distant lands, eventually ending up all the way in the civil-war-weary streets of America. He changed his name, learned the language, and did his best to fit in. The country was reinventing itself and needed men who were mechanically minded. It fit him perfectly.

He had always loved machines, and for many years he worked for an arms manufacturing company. In time of peace, this had not bothered him much. The ammunition he produced was used for hunting and sport. What found its way into criminal hands was not his fault. It was the vagaries of fate. He felt no remorse for that.

But the events of the Great War in Europe started haunting him when he discovered his company was providing arms and ammunition to the Russians.

He was a pacifist at heart, always had been and still was. Martin felt that war was the last resort of the barbarian, the only tool of the animal. He wasn't above fighting to defend himself.

He wasn't averse to self-preservation. What he was averse to, and found repugnant, was the wholesale slaughter of innocents for the sake of a few ambitious men's goals.

He stood on the platform trying to figure out what to do with his life. He couldn't go on working at the plant, but he had limited skills. He considered working as a mechanic on the railroad lines. Maybe he could get a job working on the new flying machines. Or maybe work on the Ford assembly lines. He stood watching the trains and wondering which one to take to the new life he had to create.

Mason had walked up to him and stood quietly beside him for several moments.

"Life has a way of demanding change," Mason said as if to himself.

"Pardon?"

"I noticed you watching the trains. You are trying to figure out where to go with your life."

"Do I know you?"

Mason smiled. "Not yet."

And that was the beginning.

His pacifism hadn't really been a stumbling block to his joining the Army. In his opinion, he was protecting the deceived, championing the truth, fighting for a liberty that superseded his own. Where he could never rationalize fighting in the Great War or the World War that followed, he found no difficulty in participating in the Conflict. As a member of The Army, he was stepping up against the very root of everything driving men to war: the Deception, the idea that one can make the world better by destroying a part of it. It was that dedication Mason recognized, what drove him to consider Mason's invitation to join The Army.

He hadn't accepted it immediately. After all, it was a lot to take in. A massive underground Conflict against all that was defined as good and wholesome in the world, and this was supposed to be right? He had taken his time, years searching and probing and inquiring before finally coming to the harrowing conclusion that what Mason had told him was true. Mad. Insane. Incredible. Unbelievable. And true.

He had never again doubted anything Mason told him. The man seemed to be incapable of untruth. Still, a bit of unease wouldn't allow him to commit.

Then the bombs fell on Hiroshima and Nagasaki.

All doubt about anything Mason maintained dropped away from him. All vacillation ceased. He found the man and told him he wanted to help, however he could. Since then, he had used his talents with machines and later with computers to do one thing and one thing only: to expose the Deception and fight The Enemy.

He found his mind clearing, awakening, focusing as never before. In a flash he knew he'd had a Vision, like the ones the other Knights talked about. He felt a presence inside that whispered assurance to his spirit. A surge of strength washed through him. He felt the hilt of a weapon in his fist, the weight of a shield on his arm. In the game, his avatar was a high-level fighter. That was no longer just a fantasy. In this place, the original creation where everything began, he was reborn.

He knew without looking that he was now heavily armored, his body combat-hardened and muscular. Gone was any trace of the weakness that kept him shackled to the wheelchair. He fairly shouted with new found confidence and determination.

He grinned as the woman's eyes widened in surprise, then narrowed. He beat the front of his shield with the flat of the sword in the time-worn signal of challenge.

"Come to me," the Knight Maachen said, his voice a low growl.

The beast lunged forward.

* * *

"We can't look for Martin until we find a new safe house," Jaelon was saying.

The van sped along the aging highway that once boasted the label of Interstate 40. Mason drove while Malthusan rode shotgun. The others rode in the back, with Populus at the controls of the van computers to monitor for pursuit or any evidence of hostile activity nearby.

Few private vehicles ventured onto its broken surface. It, like most roads outside the metroplexes, was falling into disrepair. Nearly all commercial travel was via air or rail now. Most people couldn't afford vehicles that could travel more than 100 miles without recharging. The governments had discovered restricting private travel helped in controlling the population, and so had all but made it impossible for the average worker to buy anything but an electric or hydrogen powered car with very limited range. Ostensibly, this was to protect the environment from pollution. High sounding propaganda campaigns and programs in public education indoctrinated the populace from childhood to accept the concept that it was unsafe to travel outside the metroplexes. Corporations built and maintained housing for their employees, so there was little need for commuting. Basic needs like food and clothing were provided through corporate and government programs. Enforcement units patrolled the areas between the metroplexes, levying stiff fines and jail sentences against those traveling without the proper authority. Passes were expensive and difficult to attain even by the corporations, much less private individuals.

Humanity in general had become complacent cattle with a few highly placed individuals as their shepherds. Most of those shepherds' offices reeked of lilac.

"We can't just give up on him," Meeker insisted. "He's one of us."

"I'm not suggesting we do," Jaelon refuted.

"I agree with Jaelon, Ms. Meeker," Populus said. "However, we could set up a mobile base to make a cursory search for his whereabouts through the Catalina Industries interface."

"Let's do that, then," Meeker said excitedly.

"Wait, wait," Overguard inserted. "Didn't you say Nicholson knew about the last time you did this? Won't he be ready, have changed his passwords or something?"

"Indeed," Populus agreed. "So, we will have to go in someplace else in the interface."

"Where else can we get in?" Overguard asked.

"The security channel," the Greek said with a grim smile.

The other two exchanged uneasy glances.

Overguard cleared his throat. "You're kidding, right?"

"Not at all. Security channels are designed mainly to monitor all the other systems' activities and user access. Often the least secure are the security channels because theoretically they have the fewest, most trusted users. If I can set just one keylogger in their frame, we'll be able to jack in and use their own systems to find Martin and maybe some of the other answers we need."

"We shouldn't stay this exposed," Malthusan said. He leaned forward to scan the sky ahead and the forests and fields that sped by from his position in the front passenger seat. "We should stop and travel only at night."

"There is an exit about three miles up that leads off into a rural area," Populus told them. He manipulated a control beside him on the van computers. One of the monitors displayed a map of the area. "There will be enough cover there."

"Right," Mason said, swinging the wheel to avoid a particularly huge pothole. His arms and hands ached from the continual pounding that traveled up the steering from the road. He was already missing the peace of his Tennessee home. It had served him for nearly sixty years, a refuge and solace from the Conflict. He grimaced as he thought of what a single

Minion had cost him in the last few weeks. Nearly a century of peace broken for the sake of Azazel's ambition. Why hadn't he listened to Azrael and left it alone?

"What about the satellite hook up?" Jaelon asked Populus.

"Still working on it," the Greek replied. "I have a lock on three right now. Want another two before I can jack in safely."

The van bounced hard across several large dips.

"Sorry." Mason grit his teeth. "Can't help it."

"Just get us off this road as soon as you can," Malthusan said. "The longer we are out, the more vulnerable we are."

"I know," Mason replied. "I'm trying."

They trundled along quietly for several minutes in silence. Mason did his best to miss the worst of the road, but often he had to crawl over broken concrete or ford places where creeks had worked across the lanes. Freight hovercraft, large, slow and cumbersome as they were, passed them frequently, their horns blaring in annoyance.

"Somebody is going to report us soon," Malthusan complained.

Mason breathed a sigh of relief as he turned the van onto the exit ramp. The pavement was heavily pitted and torn, but the van negotiated it well enough to get them into a stand of hickory and oak that provided cover from routine aerial surveillance. Of course, a determined search using simple infrared equipment could still find them easily, but there was little danger of that right now.

"Put us on level ground, would you?" Populus asked, working feverishly at his station.

Mason found a spot off the road and rolled the van to a stop.

"That will do," Populus praised. He pulled the side door open and began unloading satellite equipment.

Within a few minutes their station would be ready. While the Knights worked, Mason made use of the time to find something to eat and drink. His throat was as dry as his feelings bitter. It was always hard to start over. He had done it many times in the past, but never got used to it. A new name, a new background, new arrangements to substantiate his artificial back story as proof against all but the most determined investigation by Minions and their allies. It was a lot of work, more difficult each time as the systems on which he had to imprint his new persona became more and more resistant. Having someone with Martin's computer expertise would have made it so much easier, but there was no helping that now. He hoped Martin was all right. It chafed at him that they couldn't just set off on a rescue, but Jaelon was right. Without a secure base of operation, they would do more harm than good.

"We are ready," Populus told them. He motioned to Meeker and directed her to a seat near the controls, handed her an I/O. As she slipped it around her neck, he turned to the others. "We will need at least ten minutes clear."

"Understood," Overguard said. He went to stand on the road side of the van, venturing a lingering look at Meeker. "Be careful," he said softly as he passed.

Meeker smiled wanly at him and nodded. She turned to Populus. "Let's get this over with, shall we?"

"Remember, this will not be like the last time," the Greek stated. "We will be going into security channels. There will be plenty of chances to set off alarms. Look for this glyph, or one similar." He indicated a pictograph on his monitor. "I will provide you with the exit, but try to get as far in as you can before using it."

"I will," she promised.

"When you get in, the keylogger will appear to you looking like a key or something similar. You should not have a problem recognizing it."

"How come you don't know?"

"It will adapt to the needed form to fit the proper

circuit," Populus answered. "Look for a matching object for the keylogger and operate it as appropriate."

She looked at him uncertainly. "Okay?"

The Greek frowned. "Are you certain you want to do this? Would you rather Overguard...?"

"No, I know the interface. I can do it," she assured him.

"Very well. Ready?"

She nodded. Populus' hand moved on the controls.

She blinked at the change in lighting. The peculiar landscape stretched out either side of her instead of the interior of the van. The environment no longer made her nauseated, but she didn't stop to dwell on that. There wasn't a lot of time to get done what needed to be done. They would have to be moving along soon, so she had to hurry.

She found the little exit vial in one hand and in the other she discovered a USB drive identical to the one Mason and Tripp had brought back from Panama. The inference was clear. She needed to go back into Nicholson's office, find his computer and use the drive. Populus could then use the information from it to locate Martin.

The glyphs glittered before her. She scanned down their length and found the sigil Populus spoke of. She took a deep breath and double-tapped it.

Everything went away. Literally, everything. She was suddenly suspended in a void, a featureless space. There was no sense of falling, but the disorientation of having no point of reference made her dizzy. She reached out to try to find anything to anchor herself from her vertigo.

What was she supposed to do? She looked around, trying to locate any landmarks, any glyphs, anything that might indicate a way out. The emptiness was unbroken. It began to eat into her consciousness, to make her feel that somehow she had gone blind or deaf or worse. Panic rose in her and she held it back with an effort. She was no delicate flower, she told herself. She was as much a fighter as any of the others in the cell. She reached down inside herself and drew strength from the knowledge that what she was doing was not for herself, but to find and help save Martin. She might be his only chance now. She had to remember that.

Okay. She looked around at the void again. There must be a way to access the rest of the system from here. What would the VR generator interpret it to be?

Then it struck her. Their VR generator wouldn't have any way of interpreting a security interface on an alien frame. It would depend on information input from one or more of its users. Since they had never accessed the security interface, and

Azazel had never had reason to, there was no information to present. Thus, the void.

The VR generator needed input. Very well, she would give it some.

She knew that Populus was monitoring her activity, though he couldn't literally see what she saw. He could, however, still hear her speak though she might not in this simulation. She concentrated on her true voice. It was harder than she thought to drive her larynx as it were from remote control.

"Security interface needs information," she hoped she said. "At least a door to Nicholson's office."

A seeming eternity later, a door did appear nearby. She willed herself close to it and smirked to see the PRIVATE sign guarding it. She turned the knob.

It wasn't what she expected. Before, when she entered, there hadn't been much to see. This time the office was already displayed in its opulent glory. The shock of finding it looking like that was compounded by the sound of a voice that suddenly spoke in her ear.

"I don't know how you keep getting in here, but I do know how to keep you."

And instantly she found herself in a room of about ten feet by ten feet without windows or doors. She whirled, looking for an escape. This wasn't anything like the void. This was a prison cell.

She threw the vial.

Nothing happened. The room remained around her, unchanged. She bit her lower lip and tried to think. She knew that, physically, she was still in the Knights' van with Populus. She had to hang on to that knowledge. What was it Populus told her about the alternate exit? Something about visualizing the I/O set. She imagined it there and felt its weight against her neck. She reached for it.

"Oh, no you don't," the voice barked.

Lights and patterns pulsed in the air and on the walls around her. She struggled to ignore them, but the chaotic images kept her off-balance. Her fingers touched her neck, but the I/O set was gone.

"Odd thing about virtual reality," the voice said more calmly. "You can't close your eyes. Now, in the real world, you could plug your ears against my voice and shut off the visuals easily, but here... Well, here is subject to different rules."

Nausea rose in her as the images continued to flash and flutter.

"All right!" she shouted, holding her hands up in surrender. "All right, just stop it please!"

The chaotic images softened and faded. In their place she saw the avatar she'd encountered in Nicholson's office before, walking through one of the walls into the room to stand a few feet away.

Populus was supposed to be monitoring her. Surely he must have noticed her discomfort. Why hadn't he done anything?

"You know, I have to give you credit, you and your people," the Nicholson avatar said in the voice she had been tormented by. "You got by the very best security money can buy. And fairly handily at that."

He stepped a little to one side. "Have you ever wondered what happens to a person when they die in enhanced VR?" he asked. Although the avatar's face was incapable of mirroring the menace in the voice, she heard it anyway. "The feedback causes psychological and sometimes physiological trauma. I forget the exact medical term. Suffice it to say any wound received in enhanced VR leaves its mark on the user in real life."

As he moved closer the avatar produced a large knife from its coat pocket, a knife that should never have fit there. It shifted the knife from one hand to another.

"Now, Miss Meeker, if you're a good girl, this won't have to turn ugly."

How did he know her name? Of course. He had identified her through her avatar's appearance. Stupid, stupid! Why hadn't they thought of that?

She stepped back until she was pressed up against the wall. Where was Populus? What was keeping him?

"All I want to know is who you're working for," Nicholson went on. He continued moving toward her, knife held to his side. "Is it Dorian Azrael?"

"No!"

Why did she say that? She hadn't meant to answer at all. She tried to grit her teeth together to stop her mouth opening, but it was as if she had lost control. Was this what Populus meant when he talked about avatars responding independently?

"No? Then who?"

"The Master," she blurted before she could cover her mouth.

He stopped his slow advance. "Master? What Master?"

She sank down on the floor and curled into a ball, her hands on her traitorous lips to stop them opening.

"Tell me!" He shot forward, the knife leading his thrust. "Who is your Master?"

"Him," she mumbled through her fingers. The room was fading around her. Was Populus finally coming?

"Show me his face!" Nicholson demanded.

She was so shocked and stunned at that command she had to laugh. The laughter broke her hold on her avatar, but she didn't lose the connection. Something, whether it was the AI itself or something else, took over and she felt herself stand.

"Fool," she heard herself say. "Pitiful fool. No one sees His face, not in this world. You are nothing but a pawn of The Enemy and he has turned on you just as you have turned on him."

It was Nicholson's turn to step back. "What?"

Meeker was becoming more and more aware of another presence but she couldn't place exactly where it was. She felt herself speaking again. She began to realize that whatever that presence was had reached into her avatar and taken over. She knew she ought to be alarmed. Wasn't this like possession? Or was it? If someone took over your VR avatar, was it possession?

"I know you, Andrael," the new influence said through her AI. "I know you and I pity you. However, you are fortunate. You still have a choice. It is not too late."

"What?" Nicholson stood very quiet now, the knife gone and his face reflecting the light that suddenly flooded the little room. He pulled back another step. "You're not Meeker. Who are you?"

"I am someone you should attend," her voice said, reverberating strongly, making the walls thrum with its power. "You have made the first steps toward the other side of the Great Conflict. We know your reasons, but those are past and are forgotten. You have a chance now to make a real difference."

The room opened up into the interface landscape. Nicholson looked around. Meeker couldn't tell by his expressionless avatar, but his confusion was evident nonetheless.

"How did you do that?" he said. "That's impossible!"

"Nothing is impossible," her voice said, and Meeker saw the surprise in his body language. "Isn't that what you've always said?"

"How did you...?"

"There are forces far beyond your understanding, Andrael. You have involved yourself with things you cannot understand."

Meeker felt herself regaining control as the other faded. As the presence slipped away, she felt a great sense of loss. Her heart ached for its return, to feel it beside and within her again.

The muted lighting of the Knights' van surrounded her. She could feel a tear on her cheek and warm hands on her arm. She opened her eyes.

Jaelon smiled down at her. Meeker could see Populus

working at the computer nearby, glancing anxiously her way. The others were nowhere around, but she could hear Mason and Overguard talking outside.

"How do you feel?" Jaelon asked gently.

How? She felt as if she'd just lost someone close to her. Someone as close as her own soul. She wanted to cry out in her anguish, but could only manage a strangled sob. She reached for Jaelon's hand and found it warm and strong on her arm, but not like what she'd lost. Whatever had shared her avatar had been more than flesh and blood, more than mere artificial intelligence. A slight twinge of fear rang in her as she wondered about it, but only for a second. She looked into Jaelon's eyes and saw understanding there.

"I..." She tried to find the words, but as soon as they formed in her mind they died.

"Shush, my dear," Populus said as he left the controls and came to her side. "Stay quiet for a bit."

She settled back into the seat and let herself cry.

* * *

Andrew Nicholson pulled off the I/O set with a shaking hand.

What had just happened? One moment he was in total control, the next... How was that possible? He had commissioned that security partition only yesterday. No one could have compromised it so quickly unless they knew of its existence, and the man he'd contracted to write its code was beyond reproach.

Wasn't he?

He didn't know who to trust any more. Certainly no one outside his own circle, and some of *them* were suspect. His fellows on the Board at Catalina Industries weren't to be trusted at all. There were a few underlings that might be trusted with minor tasks, but none he felt comfortable giving anything really important.

He tossed the I/O set on to the desk and leaned back in his seat with a frustrated sigh. It was then he noticed a business card. He frowned. He didn't remember it being there when he connected. He started to reach for it, but snatched his hand back when he caught sight of the name on the card.

Janice Meeker.

What the hell? He stabbed at the intercom.

"Jessie!"

"Yes sir?"

"Who's been in here?"

There was a short pause. "Sir?"

"Did you leave this on my desk?" he snapped.

"I'm sorry, Mr. Nicholson..."

"I told you never to interrupt me while I'm working!"

"But sir, you just buzzed me."

"Don't be impertinent!"

Another pause. "Sorry, Mr. Nicholson."

"Now, who left this here?" he asked again, holding his anger in check with an effort.

"Sir, I don't know what you're talking about."

"This card, bitch!" he shouted. "Who left it?"

"Mr. Nicholson, I do not..."

"Get your ass in here right now!"

She appeared in the doorway, back stiff and jaw set, the picture of restraint.

"You wanted to see me, sir?" she said coldly.

He pointed at the card. "See that?"

She walked briskly to the desk and looked at it. "Yes."

"Who put that there?"

Jessie looked from him to the card and back. "I'm sure I don't know, Mr. Nicholson."

He bolted upright. She stood straight-backed and defiant. Nicholson glared at her.

"Do you expect me to believe this card just appeared here out of thin air?" he growled.

"Sir, I don't know how the card got there," she insisted. "No one besides yourself has been in this office."

He started to yell at her to stop lying to him. Someone had to have come in while he was interfaced. How else could the card have appeared? And if Jessie hadn't seen them, what did that mean? Did they slip by when she went to the ladies'? Or was she lying to him?

He shivered to realize how vulnerable he was physically when connected to the VR. As long as his office was secure he hadn't been concerned, but now it looked as if he wasn't as safe as he thought.

"Get out," he snapped at her.

She retreated, closing the door firmly behind her.

He stared at the card. Meeker hacked his computer, and now somehow got into his office. He was definitely in over his head. And he couldn't look to Azrael for help, not with the way things were.

5

The drink made it easier, blunted the edge of the guilt but didn't stop the euphoria. He could think about the Seraph without the pain, just the gladness and joy. Why hadn't he known about this before?

Tripp poured another glass of whiskey and threw it back. What began as a home remedy for the ache from the gunshot wound had quickly turned into something much more serious. He knew it wasn't right. Every instinct born of his Puritan upbringing screamed at him to stop whenever he looked at the bottle. But then he'd remember the Seraph, and he'd forget about that.

The guilt was still there. Every little sin still rang in his conscience, from the childhood idiocies to the killings in war, provoked and not. Seeing the Seraph brought everything to the forefront. Nothing remained hidden. How absolutely terrifying it had to have been for the Minion to face that square on.

As stunningly horrible as the exposure of all his guilt had been, the warmth and peace that flowed through him at the knowledge of how his faithfulness to the Truth had been enough to make up for it was something he yearned to feel again. Who wouldn't want to know that all their actions in their life were justified?

There had to be a way he could see it again. Some way that didn't include being on the wrong side of it, that is. He hated to think what that would mean.

All those years in The Army, and he'd never known exactly what it would be like to see the true face of his side of the Conflict. Oh, he often saw the face of The Enemy, at least of its lackeys and even a Minion now. He had stood beside Mason before he was named Mason, long before. In all that time he never imagined he would ever see what he saw that night. It was all he could think about.

The guilt of his past rumbled in his mind again. He took another drink. A gentle haze was settling over him.

How much good was he to The Army any more, anyway? They got the bullet out, but he was out of commission for a while. Mason already as much as told him he couldn't keep his mind on task, and Tripp wasn't sure that wasn't right.

He took another drink and refilled the glass.

There were only a couple of ways he could think of to see the Seraph again. One was to become what Azazel had been, a willing ally of The Enemy. He had to laugh at that. Having fought against them for so long, having seen what they did to their lackeys, after watching the results of their scheming and the lives it cost, how could he do that?

He sighed. The weight of all those things he had seen, all the things he'd done, and what no doubt awaited him in the future seemed to press in on him. He gasped and took another drink.

The killing, the spying, the constant running. What was he doing? Why did fighting for the right mean he had to do so much that seemed wrong? What difference was there between The Army and The Enemy, anyway? Didn't they both use the same tools? Didn't they both have the same goal? Weren't they both trying to accomplish the same thing?

Would whoever won this Conflict be a better ruler than the other?

He stared into the distance and listened to the echo of that thought.

"I guess it's time to think about another line of work," he said to himself. "They ain't gonna like it."

He didn't say it out loud, but he figured if they didn't, they could go visit The Enemy.

* * *

"Think about what you're doing, John," Mason said. "You don't have to do this."

Tripp shook his head and grimaced. "You don't understand," he said. "Of every one of us, you should, but you don't." He looked at Overguard, who glared at him. "I wouldn't expect you to know," Tripp told the big man. "You didn't see it. You'll never see it." A haunted look came over him. "I can't get it out of my mind," he said, almost to himself.

"John, the time will come when it will just be a faded memory," Mason assured him. "It will just be a pleasant image, like the sunset on the ocean or the sight of a ship at full sail..."

Tripp burst out laughing. "Like there's even a comparison!"

"If you step away from this cell, Tripp, you will forfeit all you have," Jaelon said grimly. "You walk away from all the good you could do in His service, make everything you have sacrificed in this life meaningless."

Tripp turned a stony face to her. "Don't talk to me about

sacrifice," he growled. "I've done my time just on the strength of a promise. I risked just as much as you, maybe not for as long, but with as much faith. When I saw the Seraph, I finally knew for sure, for certain, what I was fighting for." He looked at Mason. His visage softened and he sighed. "I'm tired, Jonah. I never understood just how tired I was until after I saw it. I'm not like you or Jaelon or the other Knights here. I don't need to prove myself. I just want some peace."

Mason wanted to argue with him about that, but wasn't Tripp saying exactly what he himself had considered? Was it fair to stop the man doing what he often wanted to do himself?

"We all want peace, John," Mason said. "Do you think any of us enjoy this Conflict?"

"You seem to!" Tripp interrupted with a shout. He glared at the Knight. "And you? What drives you? What makes somebody want to be so deep into this war they get to be a Knight?"

Jaelon glowered and drew herself up.

"Knights!" Tripp scoffed. "You're just the pointy end of the spear, aren't you?" he said with a scornful snarl.

"We serve Him," Jaelon said, coldly.

"So do we," Tripp shot back. "But we're just the ones in the trenches, aren't we? The expendable troops?"

"No one is expendable, John," Mason said. "No one."

"Tell that to Chandler and Martin!" Tripp answered.

An uneasy silence fell at the mention of their fallen comrades' names.

"Is that what this is about?" Malthusan said. "Are you afraid to die, Tripp?"

Mason put his hand out to stop Tripp charging the big Cypriot.

"If I was afraid to die, do you think I would still be with The Army?" Tripp argued.

"No one is questioning your courage," Mason said, glaring at Malthusan. The Knight returned his look dispassionately. "We're just trying to understand."

"What's to understand, Mason?" Tripp replied. "I'm done. I'm retiring. I just want to live out my life in some quiet out-of-the-way place and pass on in my sleep like a normal person. What's wrong with that?"

The company looked at Mason. He felt the full responsibility of his station as leader of the cell, and with it the pall of the knowledge he had to honor Tripp's decision.

Every man makes a decision some time in his life that defines who he is and who he will be in his future. Mason had made that decision long ago, before ever meeting any of the others standing in the room with him. He could see now, looking into Tripp's eyes, that his friend was making that kind of decision here. A decision that, even had Mason wanted to, he couldn't object to in all good conscience. Tripp had the right to the rest of his life free from the demands The Army made on them. True, he would have to disappear and always be on his guard against discovery by The Enemy. The Army might recognize his retirement, but The Enemy never would. He would forever be considered a threat, and that was something he was willing to accept. Still, it was his decision to make.

"All right, John," Mason said, putting his hand on his friend's shoulder. "I understand, I think. Of course, I don't have to like it. But I think I understand."

"You're not going to let him go," Overguard said, stepping up.

"It's his life, Stephen. It's his decision," Mason stated. He looked again at Tripp. "I would just ask you help us through this last case before you retire."

Tripp looked around at each of them for a moment. For a moment it looked as if he would object, then he nodded slowly.

"Well," he said. "I guess I can finish what I've started, anyway."

Mason smiled and patted the man's shoulder. "Thanks."

* * *

Reports from the other Army cells poured in about the increased presence of Persian forces on the borders of eastern European nations. Skirmishes between Persian forces and national authorities increased as time went along. Populus watched the news broadcasts with concern. Behind the reporters the dome of the Capitol Building stood in the distance, a familiar landmark to millions around the world.

The city was very old now, a fading jewel in the crown of a dying idea called democracy. The expansion of the socialist states in Europe and Asia no longer considered it a threat to their existence. The real danger was coming from the growing Persian Empire. Israel was a memory, gone because its allies abandoned it to political expediency. Once that nation fell, the United States and her allies quickly lost interest in the workings of the Middle East and turned inward. This blindness to the developing Persian power was bearing fruit.

Things were progressing very rapidly indeed. This little cell they had been sent to help was more of a key to the coming events than they suspected. By attacking The Enemy from several fronts, this cell and others were involved in the largest offensive ever.

Of course, Mason and the others didn't realize this and it really wouldn't make that much difference to them if they did. Populus knew they were more concerned with Martin's fate than with the larger objective, and there was nothing wrong with that. Every life was precious and worth saving.

What he needed to do was keep them focused on pushing against Azrael's organization. The director of Andlat had unwittingly supported their efforts by abducting Martin. Not surprising since The Enemy had a history of acting without consideration of the long-term consequences. He couldn't count on Azrael remaining passive long. Eventually they would strike a nerve that would send them into direct confrontation. When that happened, they needed to be ready.

6

Nicholson returned to his office to find his secretary standing outside the door. She stopped him entering the inner office.

"Mr. Nicholson, I tried to stop them but they insisted," she said, flustered.

"Who?"

"They say they're from the main office."

A chill went through him. The main office only interfered with his operation when they did an audit or changed managerial personnel. Neither prospect held much attraction for him right now. He nodded at her and straightened his jacket before opening the door.

The two men did not rise from their places. The larger of the two was planted in Nicholson's seat behind his desk. To say the man was a giant would not be an understatement.

The business suit he wore was finely tailored to accentuate the triangular torso, the thick arms, and the muscular neck. His hair was impeccable bright red. The eyes that swung to look at Nicholson were a disconcerting shade of green, nearly gleaming emeralds.

The other man looked around as he entered. He was as nattily dressed as his companion, but Nicholson nearly stumbled at the sight of the man's face.

For the briefest of moments, he thought...

But that wasn't possible. Such things didn't exist. It must have been a trick of the light.

The computer display hung from its nanofilaments over the desk, its files open and visible. Nicholson had no idea how they could have bypassed his passwords and security lockouts, but there was nothing on the computer for them to find that might hurt him.

"Gentlemen, may I help you?" he asked.

The man behind the desk leaned back in the chair. "Mr. Nicholson?"

"Yes?"

"My name is Gordon. This is Seraldo. We were sent here by Dorian Azrael to ask you a few questions."

That chill was back at the sound of Azrael's name. If

these men came from the Director himself, it definitely bode ill for him. He cleared his throat and smiled his best.

"How is the Director?" he asked, congenially.

Gordon ignored the question. "We understand an employee of yours was recently killed."

"Um... yes. Michael Jenkins, one of my divisional managers."

"And that he was attempting to blackmail you."

Nicholson stood thunderstruck. How could they know? Had Jenkins been working for Azrael all along? A mole for the Director in his office?

"I don't know..." he started.

He choked back the rest when Seraldo stood. The motion was unnaturally fluid and boneless. Gorge rose in Nicholson's throat just at the sight of it. Instantly, he wondered why. The man looked normal. What had that simple act of standing done to him to make him feel sick?

"I don't know what you're talking about," he finished, eyeing Seraldo cautiously. "Jenkins was one of my most trusted associates."

"Trusted," Gordon said, as if turning the word over in his mind. "Yes. Trust is important, is it not?"

The question was so obviously rhetorical he didn't think

to answer it. He couldn't have done so at any rate. In a way he couldn't quite comprehend, Seraldo had come a few steps closer.

"Mr. Azrael is not certain just exactly how trustworthy some people are," Gordon went on, his voice flat and emotionless. It held no overt threat, but Nicholson knew there was more behind that statement than just words.

"I assure you, I am only interested in furthering the company's interests," Nicholson said, shuffling back half a step. It didn't seem to make any difference to the distance between him and Seraldo.

Gordon looked at the display. "The company's interests. I see. And what, exactly, would you say those were, Mr. Nicholson?"

The question confused him. "What?"

Seraldo was a few inches closer, although he hadn't seen the man move.

"Would you say the company's interests coincide with your own or is it the other way around?"

The undercurrent of threat surfaced in that question. Suddenly, Seraldo was just a couple of feet away, his eyes locked on Nicholson.

"You seem to be investing in some interesting projects in

Panama, Mr. Nicholson," Gordon said, pointing to the display. "Did you know we recently had a problem there?"

"I..." Nicholson swallowed hard and licked his suddenly dry lips. "The computers in Panama City were hacked, I admit, but nothing of real value was lost. Our IT personnel were able to fix the problem quickly."

Gordon hummed and nodded. "And did they locate the hacker?"

"No," Nicholson admitted, his mouth going dry. He could almost smell Seraldo's cologne but couldn't get his feet to move. "They are still working on that."

"I see."

Gordon came out from behind the desk and walked to stand beside Seraldo. Nicholson was startled to see Seraldo was actually standing beside the chair he was sitting in earlier.

"Well, Mr. Nicholson, I want you to know that Mr. Azrael is concerned about certain activities in your office," Gordon said. He looked around briefly then nodded to Seraldo. "Although we weren't sent to terminate these activities, we *are* under instruction to encourage you to do so. We understand there were files stolen from Panama that are now in the hands of unauthorized personnel. It should be your first priority to recover those files. So, you should know we have orders to monitor your actions towards that goal and should you not accomplish this task within the next two days, we are to take steps." He smiled, but the smile was little more than a facial twitch.

"Steps?" Nicholson asked.

Seraldo opened his mouth and a sound that could only be described as a hiss issued from his throat.

Gordon placed a hand on Seraldo's shoulder. "Please excuse my colleague's brusque manner. You see, he suffers from a rare malady known as CIPA. He is unable to feel pain, heat, or cold. This has had the unfortunate side effect of making him emotionally insensitive as well." Gordon flashed that nasty smile once more. "Usually a liability, but in our line of work, a positive boon."

"And what exactly is your line of work?" Nicholson caught himself asking.

Gordon seemed surprised. "Why, messenger of course. You might call me by the old Greek word *angelos* if you like. My colleague on the other hand... well, let's just say we're alike in many ways and different in many ways."

Nicholson nodded as if he understood, even though it made no sense to him. It seemed the thing to do and it appeared to satisfy Gordon, who turned toward the office door.

"You will be hearing from us again soon, Mr. Nicholson," Gordon said as he paced toward the exit. He paused and spun slowly to grin at him. "Very soon."

With that, he left with Seraldo in tow. Nicholson caught that odor of lilac as the smaller man passed and stepped back from it. Seraldo caught the movement. He paused just a second, looking at Nicholson as if peering into his soul. Then he, too, was gone.

Nicholson realized he had been holding his breath and exhaled. His secretary appeared at the door.

"Is everything all right, sir?" she asked.

"Fine, Jessie, just fine." He went around the desk and punched off the display. "They were just here to discuss some business. Bring us a drink, will you?"

He walked to the window and looked out at the landscape of Washington, DC. He needed time to think, to calm himself and put things in order. Andlat and its subsidiaries were moving their headquarters into cities like Tehran and Baghdad to be closer to the economic heart of the world. Catalina Industries was one of the last holdouts, but even it would be moving soon to new quarters in Riyadh.

Nicholson wondered if he would miss DC, then decided it didn't really matter where he was. In a global society connected by the interweb, businesses congregated physically more out of a psychological than a financial need. Video conferencing and virtual reality avatars obviated the necessity of close personal contact. He could run his office, his entire branch even, and never leave his apartment. Most business was accomplished exactly that way. Except for the very highest echelons and blue collar drones, companies depended exclusively on computer interfacing to operate.

Which made it all the more critical he discover how his computer was hacked and that he recover the files.

Jessie appeared beside him and handed him a whiskey.

"Are you sure everything is all right, Mr. Nicholson?" she asked, worried.

He looked at her, and for the first time since he'd hired her, actually saw her.

She was younger than he recalled. Perhaps it was because she was so efficient at her job that he'd had the impression she was older. A bit rounder than slim, mid-length dark hair and wearing those oddly shaped spectacles that were in fashion now. Her dress was muted and businesslike, but not frumpy. Not a beautiful woman, but better than plain. She actually was pleasing to the eye without being overly visible, like a bouquet of spring flowers. Surprisingly, she sported a blue rose tattoo on her neck. It didn't seem to fit her, but women often did things that mystified him. She obviously bought her fragrance from the company, though.

He shook his head and smiled. Azrael's men had given him more of a shock than he realized. He hadn't thought in those kinds of images since university. In fact, he couldn't remember looking at anyone recently in any other capacity than to size them up as business allies or opponents.

What had he become? He looked at the plaque on the wall.

"Nothing is impossible."

He had become embodied ambition, always striving and never attaining. He couldn't remember the last time he'd taken a vacation or just a few days off to enjoy the fruits of his labors. Already he was wealthier than ninety-nine percent of the world, could buy and sell entire businesses from his personal accounts. He looked out the window again. From where he stood, he was higher up than the top of that Capitol Building. It seemed appropriate. He had more power at his disposal than those men in that building. They could only influence the operations of one country. Catalina Industries nearly ran the economies of several Latin American countries and did control the economies of several African nations. As CFO, he was the *de facto* head of more than ten foreign countries. More than once he had used that power to leverage even more power, to shift more wealth and influence into his own coffers.

"Sir?"

He was staring, he suddenly realized. "Sorry, Jessie. I was miles away."

"It's all right, sir. Is there something wrong with the drink?"

He looked down at the whiskey, now warm in his hand.

"No, it's fine." He handed it back to her. "Get me more ice, will you? Thanks."

With a nod, she took the glass and left. He watched until she left, then walked back to his desk. The pressure was on. Time was running out.

* * *

He walked to the coffee shop the next morning, too preoccupied to notice the man following a half block behind. It was unlikely he would have known the man, for Dorian Azrael's organization employed thousands.

Few people realize how predictable their lives have become. Routine is comfortable because familiarity is comfortable but the comfortable often leads to vulnerability. If you have designs on someone, the best way to get to them is to watch their movements for a few days. This technique, used by individuals on both sides of the law, reveals not just the target's routine, but anyone they regularly contact who might impact your designs.

Nicholson never considered his routine. He had an entire security force to cover that kind of thing. Perhaps he should have taken a bit more interest in their briefings about personal security. If he had, he might have recognized how dangerous his routine had become. As CFO of a major corporation, he should have realized he was a prime target for abduction, even assassination.

As it was, he arrived at the same coffee shop he had patronized each morning for the last two years at his regular time. He ordered, got his coffee and pastry, sat down to enjoy them. It was then his routine was broken.

The man slipped into the chair across the table and smiled at Nicholson. Before the CFO could object, the man spoke in a pleasant, quiet tone.

"Mr. Nicholson, I believe you were instructed to recover a certain item. Do you have it?"

Nicholson stammered in confusion. "I... Who are you?"

"If you don't have the item, I am afraid I am under orders to discipline you."

"Discipline?" Nicholson laughed nervously. "What does that mean?"

"You have until sunset today," the man went on. "You will deposit the item with your personal assistant for collection tonight. I look forward to meeting... Jessie, is it?" The man stood. "Until tonight, Mr. Nicholson."

And he was gone, leaving Nicholson to sit staring at his suddenly tasteless pastry and cooling coffee.

What just happened? Had he just been bodily threatened? Surely not. This must have been a warning to expect... what exactly? The man hadn't seemed that unpleasant. Kind of amiable, actually. So, why was he trembling? Sweating? Why did he have a copper taste in his mouth?

He had to use both hands to raise the coffee to his lips. It nearly hurt to swallow. It would be a long time before he could find the strength to get up and make his way to his office.

The ride in the lift was quiet and brief. The man's words kept playing over and over in his head, each time gaining a bit more menace. By the time he stepped by Jessie without returning her greeting, those quietly spoken words were more a shout in his recollection.

Time was running out. If he could get to the files, he might still salvage the situation. He'd been a fool to send only a few men the first time. He wouldn't make that mistake again.

He contacted the Catalina Industries branch in Memphis where one of his last trusted lackeys ran security. Within just a few hours, through an intensive search of the ubiquitous surveillance cameras around the area, the van was spotted and followed as it traveled across the river to disappear in the vicinity of the Little Rock metroplex. Shortly thereafter, a squadron of Catalina security officers was winging its way westward with orders to track, pursue, and kill if necessary to recover those files. As added incentive, he let it slip that they need not return if they didn't get the files.

Waiting for word, Nicholson sat at his desk, staring out the window. The night couldn't compete with the city lights. The only difference he could see between Washington DC in daylight and Washington DC in night time from his vantage point was the darkened starless sky. A gibbous moon hung motionless in that murky heaven, crookedly smirking at him.

For the first time he began to wonder if he had made a mistake. What if he couldn't get the files? Considering his previous failures and the alacrity with which Meeker's group kept penetrating his security, wouldn't it be wise to provide for that possibility?

But where could he go to escape Azrael? A deep chill settled on him. Andlat Enterprises was one of the largest, most far reaching corporations in the world. There was nowhere on the planet it didn't have some influence. There would be no refuge, no safe haven. He would have to be on the move for the rest of his life, for he knew Azrael was not the forgiving type.

How had he ended up here, caught between two shadow organizations? All he'd wanted to do was have an edge, a little something to lubricate the wheels of promotion. Instead, he'd found himself a victim of something else. And he didn't even understand how or who all was involved.

He needed to start finding out who these players really were. Maybe if he could identify a couple of them, he could start formulating a way to get out from under.

He tapped the controls on his desk. The heads-up monitor appeared and the display lowered on its nanofilaments from the ceiling to suspend over the desk.

"Playback Jenkins feed," he commanded.

Once again he watched the final moments of his traitorous subordinate. He watched as the one identified as Jonah Mason and the three other anonymous members of his troop approached Jenkins in the darkened park. He zoomed in on Mason.

"Freeze playback." He rotated the image to examine the man more closely. "Who are you?" he asked.

He manipulated the scene to more closely examine the vehicle Mason used to arrive at the meeting. It was no help. Although larger than most freight vans, it had no identifying marks. Even Catalina Industries had similar vehicles in its fleet. He sighed. It was too much to ask it might have a logo or any kind of symbol on it to help.

"Resume."

The playback continued until the odd blanking effect obliterated the image. When the field cleared, Jenkins lay dead on the ground. Once again he was puzzled. None of the others carried any visible weapons. When they recovered Jenkins' body there had been no wounds. The verdict on cause of death was massive heart attack. Something happened in those few missing seconds to cause that, but what? And the abortive pursuit outside Memphis had generated questions as well. The third car stalled out mysteriously, nor would it ever run again although it was perfectly fine mechanically. It was as if some unknown force affected it in such a way that it simply couldn't run.

Nicholson was not a superstitious man, but it certainly seemed his luck was turning against him every time he confronted that group.

It was time he stopped depending on others to get things done. Nicholson pulled out his wallet and dug into it until he found her card. There was only an email address, no telephone. He knew better than to use his own phone. Azrael could use it to find him. He needed to find an internet cafe close by.

Time to meet the enemy face-to-face.

* * *

Dawn broke over the Ozarks. The air, heavy with the aroma of earth and greenery, wafted across the little cabin perched on the cliff above the White River. Hummingbirds fought over the blossoms in the surrounding woods while bees flew past Mason as he watched the sky brighten. He sat on the front step, stretching and inhaling the freshness, so reminiscent of times long past.

He hadn't used the cabin in years, in fact had almost forgotten it existed. He purchased it somewhere in the middle of the last century from a couple who had used it every other weekend as a getaway from the bustle of the Little Rock megaplex. The road in was long overgrown and washed in several places, no real problem for the van which negotiated the obstacles with surprising ease. Mason suspected that had something to do with Populus and his mechanizations. The building itself was a simple two-room edifice with a combined kitchen and front room separated from a back room that doubled as a bedroom and storage area.

When they arrived, they parked the van under cover of a stand of oak, stirring up several squirrels' nests and causing a family of raccoon to abandon their shelter.

There was no telling how long they could stay, but though the cabin was small it would serve them well until more permanent accommodation could be prepared. There were off the grid, with no external utility services and an electric generator fitted with an EM shield to protect it from discovery when in use. Populus worked his technical magic to connect them into the interweb anonymously, assuring him no one could trace them.

He pulled out a Montecristo and moistened the tip. The click of the cutter taking off the end of the cigar helped him settle his thoughts. He took his time lighting it, savoring the familiarity of the little ritual. There were so few things any more that he felt connected him to his past, but this leisurely smoke at a quiet time was always welcome. Tripp once tried to get him to give up smoking. Bad for his health, Tripp said. The man was probably right but Mason had developed the habit sometime in the sixteenth century. Even if he wanted to kick the habit, he doubted he could just quit. He knew there were all kinds of aids developed over the past several years and he had always intended to try one someday, but not today. Today he puffed on the cigar and thought.

Security was such a critical part of their lives that every breach was cause for deep concern, but several continued to bother him, questions that went on percolating in the back of his mind.

How did Dorian Azrael find his Tennessee home? How did Azazel crack their firewall? How much of what Azazel learned from his invasion of their systems did he share with his boss before they got to him?

Only Tripp knew of the house, but he refused to believe Tripp would betray him. It was much more likely the breach of their system firewall had something to do with that. He might never know the answers to those questions but that didn't stop him wondering.

It is an ugly truth of life that questions stay with you that will go forever unanswered. The motives of others can never be completely understood. Part of life's mystery is the fact that everyone lives in isolation from everyone else. Even those closest to you, lovers, mates, will never truly be open with their lives. Every person has secrets, things they cannot share for one reason or another. Dark secrets, precious secrets, sacred secrets, they are personal gems of fear or joy that each person holds quietly in their heart forever. Enemies, of course, will always be even more of a mystery.

But in the case of enemies, those mysteries needed to be solved and the secrets uncovered to defeat their designs.

Martin had found weaknesses in their security when preparing their new server. It must have been one or more of those weaknesses that allowed Azazel to access their VR meeting place of E-Yukon. Mason had no doubt that Dorian Azrael kept close tabs on his minions and used his prodigious resources to monitor their actions and contacts. That would eventually have led to his knowledge of Mason's whereabouts. The rest they knew.

Noises from inside the cabin told him someone else was awake. He flicked ash off the end of the cigar and stood. Time to go inside and get the next step in their new lives started.

It was Overguard bumbling in the tiny kitchen.

"Got any flour?"

"Don't keep perishables here," Mason told him.

Overguard leaned against the little counter and looked

at him.

"You *do* keep food here?" he asked, a little piqued.

Mason grinned and opened a cabinet over the counter. Inside was a large stock of canned goods and several rust-colored packages.

"Okay then," Overguard said. He pulled down a couple of the packages. "What are these?"

"Military meals. Some regular MREs, some MLRPs."

"Oh. Are they any good?"

"If you're hungry, yeah. Otherwise..." Mason shrugged. "There are some UGRBs in the other cabinet."

Overguard raised an eyebrow at him.

"Rations designed for whole groups," Mason explained. "These have heaters and trays."

"Uh huh," Overguard said, peering suspiciously at the MRE he held. "How long will we have to put up with this?"

"As long as we have to, and not a moment longer," Mason promised.

"Good morning."

The men returned Meeker's greeting. She stretched and yawned.

"My, but it's quiet out here," she said. "I had a little trouble sleeping because of it."

"Provisions are being made to move us," Mason revealed. "You'll soon sleep soundly enough."

The Knights entered and Populus set up a computer on the kitchen counter. Shortly they all set about the routine chores of early morning existence.

"Miss Meeker," Populus called.

"Yes?"

"You have mail."

7

The first person she thought to show the email was Mason, who thanked her but sent her to Populus. She found him in the back room of the cabin, crouched over the computer. The Greek read the message, then sat back thoughtfully.

"What do you think?" she asked him.

"I don't know," he said. "It could be a trap."

"But what if it isn't?"

Populus nodded. "It certainly could be to our advantage to have this Nicholson as an ally." He scratched his chin. "We should take this to the others."

Meeker agreed and in short order everyone was assembled in the little cabin's main room. Mason nodded to her and she began reading.

Ms Meeker,

I have come to realize my actions have been rash and

improper. You told me I still have a choice. May I discuss that with you directly? I look forward to hearing back from you.

Sincerely

Andrew Nicholson

"So," she said to the rest. "What do you think?"

Mason scowled. "I don't like it."

"Neither do I," agreed Overguard. "It sounds fishy."

"I think it is worth the risk," Populus put in.

All eyes turned to him.

"Consider," the Greek explained, "Nicholson, who I am sure is the one called Andrael, has tried unsuccessfully several times to recover the Andlat files. Martin has disappeared and every method we have used to locate him as also failed. Even if this comes down to a simple exchange, will it not be worth it?"

"He didn't mention Martin in the email," Tripp pointed out.

"True, but he could be holding back the fact he has Martin as a last resort," Populus answered.

"I still don't like it," Overguard repeated.

"Nor do I," Jaelon said. "However, if Nicholson truly wants to parlay, perhaps we should give it a chance."

"Anything is better than this hiding," Malthusan grumbled.

Mason nodded. "Very well. We seem to have a consensus. We set up the meeting at a safe location." Overguard started to object and he cut the man off. "The Knights will be with her. The rest of us will put up a perimeter. Nobody goes in or out while Janice and Nicholson are meeting. Objections?"

No one spoke up though Overguard still looked dubious.

"Right. There is a little town nearby called Mountain Home. I know the owner of a local bar there. Janice, send him this reply."

She wrote down Mason's directions and headed to the computer. Her heart raced as she typed in the reply. It wasn't until she reached for the "send" button that the importance of the communiqué hit her and she paused.

What if it *was* a trap? Sure, the Knights would be there, but if this Nicholson was a Minion like Jenkins had been, would she have the courage to face him? She wished she had seen them when they took on Azazel. Their ability to handle the demon in Mason's house was impressive, almost frightening.

A slight noise caught her attention. Stephen stood there, a worried look on his face. The memory of his story about Mexico came back in a rush. He was the sole survivor of that encounter. The rest of his cell was wiped out. She could see the haunted look in his eyes and knew he was thinking the same thing.

They had already lost Martin. She could see he wanted to stop her, but held back. It hurt to see him so distressed, but what else could she do? Nicholson had only ever seen her so far and she felt it was her duty to do this.

She smiled at him. "I know," she told him, answering his unvoiced concern.

After a moment, he nodded sadly and moved off to stand by a window with his back to her. She noticed Jaelon watching them both. The other woman's eyes told her she understood as well.

Meeker hit "send".

* * *

The bar was dimly lit by the old-fashioned neon signs extolling the virtues of this and that beer and soft liquor. Hidden speakers wailed a country tune she didn't recognize. The booth she occupied sat close to the door leading into the back room. Meeker sat quietly observing the barflies, mostly men in rough clothes and hard faces talking amongst themselves about sports, politics, and farming. She imagined the place hadn't changed that much since its establishment which a sign over the bar announced as 1967. The place was clean enough, but it still reeked of sweat and beer. Hardly the place one would expect to be the site of such a meeting, she thought. Then again, maybe that was why Mason chose it.

A murmur brought her attention to the front door.

Andrew Nicholson was not what she expected. His avatar only vaguely resembled the man himself. Meeker was struck by his smooth manner and boyish good looks. Somehow she had expected a much older man. He couldn't be that much older than she. It startled her that her heart actually skipped a beat as he entered the little bar. She suddenly understood how he could have risen so highly so quickly in Catalina Industries. He had a personal presence that caught the attention of every woman there.

He stopped for just a moment at the door, casting a glace around the room before settling on her. He briskly walked to her table.

"Miss Meeker?" he asked.

His voice, unfiltered by the VR interface, was softer and warmer than expected. She swallowed to clear the lump in her throat and licked her dry lips.

"Yes. Mr. Nicholson?"

"Andrew, please." He smiled and she admired his ease. "May I join you?"

Not trusting her own voice, she motioned an invitation to sit. He slid into the seat opposite gracefully.

"You and your friends have given me quite a chase," he said. "I must admit you have proven yourselves quite the able adversaries."

She nearly jumped when Mason's voice came over the subcutaneous communicator planted just behind her ear.

"Relax, Janice," Mason said. "He's alone best we can tell. Jaelon and the others have you both in sight."

"I am very glad you agreed to see me," Nicholson was saying. "Under the circumstances, I was afraid you might refuse. Not that I would blame you."

She took a deep breath. "I think it's past time, don't you?"

"Indeed." He smiled again. "I believe we have much to discuss."

"I assume that's why we're here," she answered with a smile of her own.

He looked around. "So, how many are here?"

So, she thought. Good looking and no fool either. No point in lying.

"All of them," she revealed.

That seemed to amuse him.

"Am I that dangerous?" he asked, smiling.

"I don't know," she answered honestly. "Are you?"

He leaned forward suddenly, prompting her to jerk backward. Instantly a shadow fell over the table. Meeker looked up to find Malthusan standing there, back to them and ostensibly talking to Populus. The Greek caught her eye and winked. Nicholson caught the look.

"Hello there," he said to Populus. "I believe I know you. And your large friend as well. Where's the woman?" He turned in his seat and scanned the room. "Ah, there she is at the bar." he waved congenially at her. "Gentlemen, please join us. You don't mind, do you Miss Meeker?"

The Knights took the invitation, Populus sliding in beside Meeker and Malthusan wedging his frame halfway into the seat with Nicholson.

"Now, isn't this better?" Nicholson asked Meeker. "Do you feel safer?"

"Actually, yes," she admitted.

"Good. Now, perhaps we can talk more freely. What I have to say applies to all of you, anyway."

"Exactly what does that mean?" Malthusan growled.

"Easy," Nicholson said, unimpressed. "I'm not here to threaten you. I'm here to try to negotiate the return of company property."

"Negotiate?" Malthusan scoffed.

"Yes, negotiate."

"Did you run out of ammunition?"

Nicholson grimaced. "Maybe this was a mistake after all."

"Don't let him leave," Mason said in Meeker's ear.

She reached out and put her hand on Nicholson's arm as he looked to rise.

"Please." She shot a hard look at Malthusan. "Do you mind?"

The big Cypriot glowered at her, then got up and went to sit with Jaelon.

"I hope you understand our skepticism," Populus said. "That does not mean we will not listen."

Nicholson glanced at Malthusan. "You have to look at this from my perspective, Mr...?"

"Populus."

"Mr. Populus. I came here into the lion's den, as it were, without backup or any kind of extra protection."

"And I do appreciate that, Andrew," Meeker said. "Even if the others don't."

There was that quick smile again. She found herself liking it. His face lit up a certain way when he smiled like that.

"Thank you, Janice. May I call you Janice?"

She felt herself blush. "Of course."

"I know we've been at odds until now, but I think that perhaps we can find an equitable agreement to settle our differences."

"What do you suggest?" Populus asked.

"Well, you have certain information I need. I am willing to negotiate for it."

"I see. We understand your wish to gain control of those files. You see, we also know their purpose."

Nicholson's face went carefully neutral. "Indeed?"

Populus produced a USB drive from one of his many pockets. He set it on the table. Meeker thought she heard Nicholson gasp, but she wasn't sure.

"In fact, we have taken this information one step further," Populus went on, tapping the device with his forefinger.

"You..." Nicholson frowned, puzzled.

"Jenkins intended to give you these files in exchange for money or power, am I right?"

The other man's face went neutral again. He remained silent. Populus grinned.

"Do not fear, Mr. Nicholson. We require neither."

She could see the confusion on Nicholson's face. It

reflected her own. What was Populus doing?

"You may have your files in exchange for a single promise. The same promise we asked of Jenkins."

"And that is?"

The Greek pushed the drive closer to Nicholson. "You will forget us and never reveal anything you know about us to anyone, especially Dorian Azrael."

Now Meeker was really confused. Azrael already knew about them, had met with Mason more than once. Populus' deal made no sense to her, but she tried not to let that show. Nicholson sat looking at them, then reached out and took the drive.

"I may assume the promise goes both ways?" he asked.

"You may."

"Then, done. You have my word."

He extended his hand.

A bright red spot appeared in his shoulder and blood spattered across the table. Something thumped into the seat between Meeker and Populus.

The bar erupted into chaos.

"Shooter!" Jaelon's voice echoed in her communicator.

"Get out of there!" Mason's voice responded.

The sound of gunfire echoed outside. Populus dragged

her out of the booth, shouting to Malthusan. Between them, the Knights pulled Nicholson out and carried him into the back room and outside. Meeker followed on their heels, heart pounding.

Somebody shot Nicholson! And nearly hit her!

The Knights' van rumbled up and they climbed aboard. Overguard watched them anxiously from behind the wheel.

"Where's Jaelon?" she shouted.

"Quiet, girl!" Populus hissed. He pulled the van door shut behind them. "She'll be along if she can."

"But we can't just leave her!"

"Go!" Malthusan shouted at Overguard.

The van leapt to life.

* * *

At the sound of the first shot, Jaelon barked the warning and jumped at the shooter, a woman about her age in appearance. The two women collided as the second shot went off, bursting an overhead fan. Electrical sparks showered the crowd, throwing everyone into a confused panic.

Jaelon grappled the woman's gun hand as the other tried to bring the weapon to bear. The woman reeked of lilac.

The cloying odor was nauseating, but Jaelon pushed that away. She had all she could do to hold her enemy down. In just a few moments, she knew that was a losing battle. The opponent was stronger and gained the upper hand, tumbling them both until she was above Jaelon, grinning. The barrel of the silencer inched toward Jaelon's face.

An explosion knocked the woman completely off Jaelon. The sharp stench of cordite replaced the lilac as if the latter had never existed. Stunned, her ears ringing, Jaelon rolled to see her adversary lying several feet away. As she watched, the woman twitched then rose quickly, bleeding profusely from what should have been a fatal wound in her side. The handgun had been blasted free of her grip. Unarmed, she gave Jaelon a snarl, then disappeared outside.

Jaelon started when someone touched her.

"You okay, miss?" the barkeeper said. He held a sawed-off shotgun in his hand.

"Yes, thank you," she said, struggling to rise.

"I'm real sorry I had to shoot her," the man said with a tremble in his voice. "I thought she was goin' ta shoot you."

She leaned over and kissed him lightly on the cheek. "Bless you. You saved my life."

He smiled shyly and cleared his throat nervously. "Who

was she? Did ya know her?"

"No."

"Well, that was real brave, what you did." He looked at the shotgun and his face changed. "I never shot nobody afore." He turned frightened eyes on her. "Am I goin' ta jail?"

Jaelon could see the panic rising in him. The poor fellow was just now realizing what had happened. He'd acted purely out of instinct to protect her. She put her hand on his shoulder.

"What is your name?" she asked him, her voice level and calm.

"Walter Morris," he answered.

"Walter, you will not go to jail. You were protecting me and the other people here. Anyone who saw what happened will say so."

She felt the tension flow out of the man as she spoke.

"Yeah, I was, wasn't I?"

"Of course you were. And you saved my life as well."

His back straightened just a little at that. "Yer welcome," he told her. "Warn't nuthin'."

Jaelon smiled at him again. "Now, may I ask you another favor?"

"Sure."

"I would rather not get involved any more in this. When

the police come, would you leave me out of it?"

"Guess so," he said cautiously.

"All you have to tell them is the truth. The woman shot someone and you drove her off before she could hurt anyone else."

He swallowed hard, but nodded. "Okay. Say, what happened to the guy?"

"I expect my friends have taken him to the hospital."

"Oh. Okay."

A siren began to wail in the distance.

"Remember, I was not here," Jaelon said, moving her hand from his shoulder to press gently against his chest. "You were protecting your customers."

Morris' jaw set and he brandished the shotgun. "Wouldn't be the first time, miss," he said more confidently. "You best hightail it afore the cops get here."

She gave him another kiss on the cheek. He blushed, grinning like a schoolboy.

"Thank you," she whispered in his ear.

She made her way toward the back as the siren grew. She found Mason and Tripp waiting for her.

"Nicely done," Mason said, nodding toward the barkeeper.

She shrugged. "People are at their most suggestible when under stress. I just gave him something to anchor himself while he comes to grips with what happened."

"That's nice. We need to go," Tripp said impatiently.

An unfamiliar small green car stood at the back door. Jaelon gave the men a questioning look.

"Don't ask," Tripp said. "Just get in."

They set out for the cabin.

* * *

Populus and Malthusan were already taking care of Nicholson when they arrived. The Knights had pulled a bed into the front room and put Nicholson on it. They had him hooked to an IV. Meeker stood watching them, fascinated.

"It's amazing," she told Mason as he came in. "They closed the wound just by laying on their hands!"

"Nothing you yourself could not do with the proper training," Jaelon said, pushing around them to stand by the other Knights.

"Really?" Meeker said, mouth agape. "Really?"

"How is he?" Mason asked.

"The bullet passed through," Populus answered. "It

hit nothing vital. He will be sore for a while, but should fully recover. The equipment from the van will counteract his loss of blood and we have pumped him full of antibiotics and pain killers. He will need to be watched for at least twenty four hours for signs of shock."

"I don't understand how they got by us," Overgaurd said, shaking his head.

"It was a Minion," Jaelon told them.

Everyone looked at her in shock.

"You got a good look at it?" Mason asked.

"Oh yes. It almost killed me. Luckily, the bartender is a good shot."

"He killed the host?" Populus gasped.

"No, just wounded her," Jaelon responded. "She left under her own power before I could stop her."

"I don't know if that's good or bad," Tripp said.

"Obviously Nicholson was the target," Mason observed. "Most likely the shooter was working under orders from Azrael."

"That puts Azrael's agents uncomfortably close," Overguard gloomed. "I told you I didn't like it."

Nicholson moaned. The women went to stand by his bed. His eyelids fluttered open and he focused on them. He made to sit up, but fell back again with a groan.

"What happened?" he managed to croak.

Meeker knelt beside him and took his hand. "Rest. You need to rest."

He looked around, alarm growing in his face. "Where am I? What did you do to me?" He tried again to rise quickly, but this time the exertion of the movement and his outburst proved too much and he collapsed into unconsciousness again.

Meeker swung to Mason. "What do we tell him?"

The Angelkiller stood looking down at Nicholson for several moments. Meeker wished she could see the thoughts that must be racing through his mind. He finally seemed to come to a decision.

"We can't keep him here, nor can we take him with us," he said.

She was horrified at his meaning. "We can't just walk away. They'll kill him."

"What choice do we have?" Overguard argued. "We've lost Martin because of him. Guarding him could get the rest of us killed."

She gaped at him. Was he agreeing to this? "We can't just abandon him."

Overguard started to say something then stopped.

He looked from her to where she held Nicholson's hand. She realized just before she shifted her hand to her side what he must be thinking.

Was he jealous? Was that why he wanted to leave Nicholson to his fate? Was Stephen that insensitive, that self-centered? She never thought so. Could she have been so wrong about the man? He must have been more fragile emotionally than she thought. She knew about his guilt over being the sole survivor of his Mexican cell, but she'd hoped he was learning to cope with it.

She rose and walked toward him, intending to say something to reassure him of her feelings, but he turned away and walked out of the cabin. The hurt in his eyes told her more than any words he could have uttered.

"Miss Meeker is right," Jaelon said, breaking the tension in the room. "We have him now for good or ill."

"Fine," Tripp grumbled. "How do we convince *him* of that?"

"You let me take care of that," Populus said.

"We still need to find Martin," Tripp retorted. "He's our only lead."

"Then I will have to be very persuasive," the Greek stated.

"You won't hurt him?" she worried.

Populus looked insulted. "My dear, what do you take me for?"

"How soon can he be safely moved?" Mason asked.

"Give it a couple of hours. We should have him stabilized by then."

Mason nodded. "Keep him under until we can get him someplace safe away from here."

"Understood."

8

The Manchester Arms was a parody of the dignity of its name. Crouched between an abandoned building that might once have been a restaurant but was now the dwelling place for dozens of rats and an adult book store that bore a striking resemblance to the former restaurant, the Manchester was definitely showing its age. The front window was long broken and covered with a thick plate of fiberboard. The main door always stood at least a half inch open because the door frame was warped. The lobby, what there was of it, smelled of moldy furniture and cheap liquor processed through the bladders of several of the room's denizens, none of whom were paying clients, but the landlord seldom visited until later in the day. The rooms were small and claustrophobic, with worn furniture and threadbare rugs.

Nicholson woke slowly, fighting off the drugs that

worked to keep him senseless. He could hear voices nearby. It was Meeker and the one he assumed was the other woman in the group speaking quietly. He feigned being asleep and listened.

"He is lucky to be alive," the woman said.

"What about me!" Meeker said.

"Yes, you as well."

"I've never been so scared, Jaelon. When that bullet hit him, I thought..." He heard her sob.

"I know, my dear."

"Why would they try to kill him? Wasn't he working for them?"

"I suspect he may be working for himself. We know Azazel was working for him and against Azrael."

"Azazel was working for himself," Meeker countered a little hotly.

"Yes, but it appears from what we know now that he and Nicholson may have been plotting against Azrael."

Nicholson was confused. Who was Azazel? He didn't know anyone by that name, certainly not in his employ. It wasn't the kind of name he'd forget if he heard it.

"The woman that shot him did not have time to make sure the job was done," Jaelon was saying. "Someone is sure to follow up and try again if necessary."

So, a woman shot him, someone they didn't know.

"Maybe he can tell us something about who she might be when he wakes up," Meeker suggested.

"I do not think he saw her."

"But you did."

"True, and I would certainly know her should I see her again."

Nicholson had heard enough. It was obvious they weren't involved in the attack, but they could identify his would-be killer. He opened his eyes and shifted. Pain shot through him. His shoulder ached horribly bone-deep. He grunted through clenched teeth. The women appeared standing over him, Meeker looking worried and solicitous, Jaelon more curious than concerned.

"Stay still," Meeker told him.

"Kind of have to," he answered. As the pain subsided, he was surprised to find his other senses greatly heightened. Maybe it was the drugs, maybe it was simply the knowledge of how close he had come to dying. There was a funny taste in his mouth and his teeth needed brushing. Someone was wearing a rose-scented perfume. Water dripped in a metal sink. "Where are we?" he asked, unwilling to move again to see for himself.

"In a safe place," Jaelon said. She stopped Meeker when the woman would have added to that.

He didn't miss Jaelon's action. "I see," he said, grimly. "What happened?"

"What do you remember?"

Good question, he thought. The conversation in the bar was clear enough, the shot was unforgettable, then something about the group in a small room that smelled of fresh cut wood and greenery. A cabin? A shed? The memory was too fuzzy to be real, but it definitely wasn't here.

"Not much after the shot," he admitted. "I guess you patched me up?"

"Populus did," Meeker told him.

"Well, tell him thanks for me." A sudden unsettling thought occurred to him. He was feeling pretty good to have just been shot. That wasn't something that happened in a couple of hours. "How long have I been out?"

"Two days."

His heart sank. Two days. Too late. There was no going back now. He wouldn't put it past Azrael to have put the hit on him, knowing if he did survive it would only delay the inevitable. Nicholson lay looking at the blank ceiling of the room. So much had gone so wrong so quickly. He knew when he started this there would be risks, but until now he never truly understood what those risks might entail.

Someone was really trying to kill him.

It was a hard thing to take in, that Azrael would consider him such a threat that only death would neutralize it. Surely they might have come to some kind of agreement? They were both businessmen, after all. And hadn't this all been about business?

What was he going to do? He'd hardly considered the possibility of failure. He wasn't accustomed to it. He'd had setbacks, true, but this was more than just a setback. Much more.

"Are you in a lot of pain?" Meeker asked. "Would you like me to..."

"No, no thank you. Just considering my situation and finding my options a bit limited. I am quickly coming to the conclusion that I am in over my head here, but what can I do about it?"

"Let us help," Jaelon said. "We need someone inside Andlat. You need to get free of Azrael. It is a mutually beneficial agreement."

Nicholson hesitated in thought. If he refused, he would definitely be on his own. The two days they had given him to recover the files was up. He didn't know what waited for him back in Washington, but he was sure it was nothing pleasant.

Joining this group, these people who had somehow managed to thwart him at every turn, would at least give him a fighting chance. He still didn't know much about them, but they were definitely not out to kill him and that was a plus in their column.

"I guess I don't really have much choice," he said at last. "I either join you or face Azrael's goons."

"Wonderful!" Meeker said, happily. She gripped his hand tightly.

He was a bit startled by her touch, but recovered quickly and smiled at her. She blushed and dropped his hand, turning away to cover her nervousness. She was an attractive woman, and she seemed to be attracted to him. He wondered...

"The next step is to formally introduce you to the group, I suppose," Jaelon said. "Miss Meeker you already know. My name is Jaelon."

He sighed at the thought. "It will be interesting to finally meet the people I've been trying to eliminate for weeks," he said wryly. "I hope there are no hard feelings."

"I cannot speak for everyone," Jaelon said. "Personally, I have no ill will against you."

There was a knock at the door. Jaelon went to look who

was there, then opened it.

"Andrew Nicholson, this is Jonah Mason," she said.

Mason paused at his bedside. The men silently regarded each other.

"Mr. Mason," Nicholson said solemnly. "Nice to finally meet you in person."

"Andrael," Mason said.

Nicholson started, and immediately regretted the movement. This group knew more about his operation than he had imagined if they knew his operational alias.

"I wanted you to know we had nothing to do with your shooting," Mason told him.

"I believe you," he told the man.

That surprised him. Mason frowned and glanced at Jaelon, who shook her head in answer to his unspoken question.

"Well," Mason said hesitantly, "I'm glad. We will shortly be moving you to a safe location. We have taken the liberty of searching you for locator devices. Do you have any idea how the shooter found you?"

He shook his head slowly. "Honestly, I didn't trust anyone knowing where I was going."

"I see. So you left no evidence behind that might hint at your destination?"

"Nothing."

Mason nodded thoughtfully. "Well, I will leave you with Jaelon. If you remember anything, don't hesitate to let us know. We can't protect you if you keep secrets from us."

"Understood."

The two stepped away to speak in low tones together. Meeker came back to his side.

"You really should rest," she said. "The others will be here soon to carry you to the cabin."

"Okay." He reached out and took her hand. "I just want to thank you for saving my life."

She blushed. "I didn't do anything. It was Populus."

"I don't mean the gunshot. I mean showing me there is more to life than ambition." He smiled. "I'm beginning to understand there is more to this than I first thought."

She glanced at the two standing nearby. "I wonder..." She looked back at him. "If you are going to be with us, you should know the truth."

Nicholson listened in increasing disbelief as she described the Conflict between The Army and The Enemy. He found it hard to believe, but maybe Meeker was right. Maybe Azrael was part of a bigger, more complex organization and he'd just stung it in the wrong place at the right time. The whole thing about fallen angels and clandestine armies was a bit much, but in essence her story was looking more and more like as good an explanation as any for what was happening to him.

Sometime during Meeker's narrative Mason left and Jaelon came to stand beside them.

"I understand you fought with the person who tried to kill me," he told her.

"I did. I am only sorry I did not see her sooner."

He waved away her apology. "Could you describe her to me?"

Jaelon thought for a few moments. "Stoutly built, with dark hair cut to the shoulder, about my height."

As she went on, Nicholson's heart raced. The description was too familiar.

"Did she have any body art?" he asked.

"Excuse me?"

"Tattoos. Did she have any tattoos?"

"Come to think of it, she did. I saw some kind of flower on her neck. I think it was a blue rose."

That clinched it. "Jessie," he said.

"You know her?"

He plopped down on the bed, head suddenly spinning.

"She's my personal assistant." And now there could be no doubt.

Azrael was trying to kill him.

* * *

They carried him back to the little cabin in the mountains, the place he had vaguely remembered as in a dream before. Nicholson was surprised to find himself feeling so much better with each passing moment. He wouldn't have believed he could recover so quickly from a gunshot.

He learned much in the following hours about the Conflict and its players. He learned about Angelkillers and Minions, the Army cells and the Enemy strongholds, the Light's network of resistance and the Dark's imbedded presence in governments and corporations. The more he heard, the more things made sense: the growing political and social unrest in the world, the increasing displacement of spiritual influence in law making, the concentration on humanism in judicial decisions. He had to admit they made a strong argument, and his recent personal experience only further strengthened their contentions.

He was quickly introduced to the rest of the group

because Populus was pressing the need to act on Martin's disappearance. Nicholson had only ever seen a picture of Martin, but he understood their concern over the man's abduction, considering what he knew of Azrael's methods. The group gathered in the little front room of the cabin to plan.

"The best way to find out where they have taken Martin is to go back into the system and implant a tracker," Populus briefed them. "Behind that, we will implant a botnet that will wipe out not only the evidence of our presence, but shut down Catalina Industries."

"Considering we already crashed their system once, they're going to be extra cautious," Tripp said.

"True," the Greek responded. "However, we now have the answer to that. Mr. Nicholson."

He raised up on his elbow. "Yes?"

"We will need your help. Are you willing?"

He felt the gaze of every person there, but felt no pressure to decide from anyone but Overguard who scowled deeply at him. Why that man in particular? The ones called Knights, Mason, and Tripp watched expressionless. Meeker looked at him hopefully.

Was he willing? For now, it seemed he had little choice. Somewhere down the road he might rethink his decision, but for right now...

"Yes," he agreed.

"Excellent," Populus said, rubbing his hands together. "Now, let us get down to the job of finding Martin and shutting down The Enemy."

9

Nicholson had a sudden twinge. It had taken him three years to build Catalina Industries up to what it was. Destroying it, even as a side effect of taking down Andlat, seemed wrong. He understood their reasoning. He knew he could never again sit in that Washington office. Still...

He shook himself. It was just a business after all. Businesses came and went, whether or not by design. The majority of what had been Catalina Industries would be absorbed back into Andlat, and wasn't that the point? Catalina Industries was just the first step in the process to bring Azrael out from under his master's protection. Once exposed, they might – *might* be able to deal with him as they had Azazel.

It was so odd to find he had employed a Minion. Jenkins had been abrasive and a bit of an ass, but that didn't differentiate him from any of a hundred other men in similar positions. There needed to be a little shark in you to set you apart from the herd.

Most people are content to be led, to be told how to live their lives because it was easier to let someone else make the hard decisions. The fear of failure, inbred into every human being and better identified as the instinct for self-preservation, made the greater part of humanity just so many sheep. Nicholson knew that simple fact and had used it repeatedly over the years to lever himself higher in business. A kind word here, a veiled threat there, and another rung on the ladder achieved. Confrontation or just the threat of it was a powerful tool. People would go a long way, allow much, sacrifice some to avoid confrontation. It was the most insidious, most subliminal, most effective manipulator of the self-preservation instinct.

A manipulator they hoped would work against Azrael.

The office VR was remarkably accurate from this system. He found himself admiring their expertise even as he was annoyed at the ease at which they accessed his own system. So much for the best IT money could buy. Whoever created this interface was light-years ahead of anything he'd seen.

Meeker's avatar turned toward him.

"Something wrong?" she asked.

He didn't answer, just walked to the desk. It was a fair replica. Not as ornate, but containing all the critical controls.

He tried to pull up the office files, but a featureless humanoid suddenly appeared. It gazed eyeless at them.

"Identify please," it said.

"Andrael," he told it.

"Identification failed. Identify please."

"Damn, they changed the passwords already," he mumbled.

"Surely you have a quick access code? Something you can use from a portable device, maybe?" Meeker asked, though he supposed she was being prompted by Populus.

"Come to think of it..." He turned back to the humanoid. "Andlat is mine," he said.

Instantly they were surrounded by a multiplex of rooms representing the entire contents of his computer. Seen this way it was impressive and not a little confusing. He was a bit overwhelmed.

"Wow," Meeker said.

"Yeah," he agreed.

It took a few minutes to decipher the system icons. He wished he'd paid more attention in university. He might have found the necessary files more quickly. He kept glancing at Meeker, who was slowly becoming visibly bored. He found that made him uncomfortable. Did he really want to impress her that badly?

There it was, the opening Populus talked about. He looked at the item in his hand and at the receptacle. No sense in prolonging the moment. He was out of options. This was all he had left. He placed the key in its place. It slowly dissolved as if melting in a forge.

"It's done," he announced when it was fully gone.

Meeker smiled. Hard to believe an avatar could do that. Maybe he just thought he saw that. Maybe it was just a trick of perspective. Were the enhanced I/O's inputs affecting his perception?

"We best get back," she said. "Do you need a guide out?"

He didn't really. "Yes, if you don't mind," he told her.

She took his hand and they made their way out. He was sorry when the simulation ended and he found himself once more in the company of the Greek alone.

"Well done," Populus said as he monitored the progress of the worm. "The watchtower programs are ignoring it. The botnet will rebirth throughout the system within a few seconds." He looked at Nicholson. "Catalina Industries is now down permanently and Andlat is crippled. It will take them months to recover. They are not completely out of operation. We did not want them to resort to desperate measures that might cause innocents to suffer. However, much of their hardware will be unusable and will need to be replaced or rebuilt from scratch." He bowed his head to Nicholson. "Well done, sir."

Nicholson felt numb. In a single stroke he had destroyed everything he had built. Shouldn't he feel something, anything? All he could think of was what Azrael was going to do. Would he know who was behind the crash? Populus' assurances that it was untraceable aside, how true was that of anything?

He was going to have to start over, but he was young and smart. Starting over didn't frighten him. It was the thought of his past catching up that bothered him. He had traded his past for a new future. It wasn't until just that moment that the reality of how badly that past could haunt his future occurred to him.

"Something is bothering you," Populus observed. He turned in his seat to face Nicholson. "You did the right thing."

Nicholson nodded shortly. He trusted this group more than his former employees. At least he knew these people weren't trying to kill him.

But how much better of a gauge of trustworthiness was that, after all?

Suddenly the cabin seemed cramped and stuffy. He pulled the I/O set off and stood.

"I need some air," he said.

The Greek nodded, taking the I/O from him. He walked past Meeker, who stood with Mason, reporting what she'd seen. She smiled at him and he did his best to smile back, but couldn't manage much. It wasn't her fault. None of this was any of their fault.

Now that it was done, he found he could step back and look at all that had happened with new eyes. He back-traced the sequence of events to its origin and found himself as the prime mover. Of course, he always knew that. It was simply easier to blame someone else. Someone like Jenkins. Or Meeker. Anyone but the real culprit.

He walked down the few steps to stand in the little front yard overgrown with dandelions and clover. To his left the ground fell away into the river. The sound of the water was soothing. Frogs croaked on its banks. A cricket sang briefly. Someone was talking inside, but he heard nothing more intelligible to him than the cricket's song.

He closed his eyes and tried to blank his mind. Forget it all. Forget them all. Forget what he had done. Forget what might be. Just listen to his own breathing, to this moment, to the beginning again.

And it was so quiet. All his life had been filled with noise, the hum of the Machine of Civilization working 24/7, a constant background, a constant companion. It was so odd not to hear that low tone underneath everything else. It never dawned on him just how alien that sound should be, how it tapped into his subconscious, enslaving his id to its continual patter.

Was that what drove him so? Was his ambition nothing more than a desperate need to escape that ubiquitous subliminal thunder? Separated now from it, he couldn't find that burning desire to have more, to grab at the brass ring always just outside his reach.

Was it possible that all along he had only ever wanted this quiet peace?

He took a deep breath, inhaled the scent of pine, a clean smell unlike the artificial parody manufactured by laboratories to convince people who never stepped outside the boundaries of steel and concrete that they knew what nature smelled like. There really was no comparison. There was life in this, not in the other.

He opened his eyes.

The green around him had brightened. The birdsong was more clear, the singing of the frogs somehow more musical. It was as if a veil had lifted from his senses. The fear was gone.

He felt reborn.

* * *

Overguard stood at the cabin window watching Nicholson in the front yard. Since meeting him, Janice had been distant. Could she feel something for the man? Overguard fought with that thought. Janice and he shared a special tie, didn't they? Nicholson was handsome in his own way, he supposed, but did that mean Janice was...?

He crossed his arms and frowned. He didn't like this feeling. Janice wasn't his property. She was a beautiful, intelligent woman who surely saw through the glamor surrounding Nicholson. She wouldn't be taken in by something as shallow as good looks, would she?

He looked at her, talking to Mason. He felt a tightening in his chest.

Should he ask her? Should he just walk up to her and ask her straight out how she felt about Nicholson?

No. He couldn't do that. What if she did? Did he really want to know? What could he do about it?

The door opened and Nicholson stepped inside. Their eyes met and he stopped, looking at Overguard with what seemed to be cool appraisal. Overguard returned the look with one of his own. Did the man think he could be intimidated that easily?

Nicholson broke contact and went into the back room. Overguard caught Janice watching him go by. He wanted to think it was the natural instinct each person has to follow movement until its origin was identified, but Janice went beyond the cursory glance. She turned to the man, who ignored her, and looked uncomfortably disappointed at the snub.

Who was this guy to walk into their lives and disrupt things? He'd tried to kill them more than once. For all they knew, he was responsible for Martin's disappearance. He wasn't to be trusted, that's for sure.

"Everyone," he heard Mason say. "Gather 'round please. Populus has some news."

"Something about Martin?" Janice asked hopefully.

"Afraid not, my dear," the Greek replied. "It is bad news. Apparently the botnet was unable to penetrate farther than Catalina Industries' computers. The security measures in Andlat Enterprises' network stopped it before it could get in."

"So we didn't do any good at all?" Tripp asked.

"We did. Catalina Industries is more than likely not going to recover for some time, and many of its subsidiaries are in trouble. Unfortunately, this gets us no closer to finding Martin or stopping Andlat. The Catalina network had nothing on Martin's whereabouts. If anyone knows about him, the information is locked away in Andlat."

"You thought I was responsible for this Martin's disappearance?" Nicholson scoffed. "I admit I tried to recover the Catalina files, but I had no idea this Martin was even missing."

"You gotta admit you looked good for it," Overguard broke in. "You *have* been trying to kill us."

Nicholson acknowledged the charge with a little bow of his head. "Yes. I have already admitted to that. But I did not abduct your friend."

"Maybe you know who did."

"I do not. I have nothing to do with it."

"That's enough," Mason barked. "The important thing now is to get into Andlat and see if we can find anything about Martin."

"And take down Andlat," Tripp added.

"That's a given," Mason agreed.

"That may not be as easy as it has been up to now," Populus announced.

"Like anything has been easy up to now," Tripp scorned.

"However," the Greek went on, ignoring Tripp, "I do have a plan."

10

"The Andlat computers are controlled by The Enemy," Populus explained. "No doubt they have been modified to detect the botnet we used at Catalina and stop it infecting the system. However, I seriously doubt Andlat has been able to do much more than that. Their watchtowers may recognize it, but the system itself would still not know how to purge it. Identification and elimination are two different processes."

"So, if you get past the firewalls and watchtowers, the botnet could still work," Mason surmised.

"Exactly."

"How do you propose to do that?"

Populus held up his hands, palms forward. "Watch." His hands began to glow very slightly. "This ability is most often used to heal injury, as we did with Mr. Nicholson. It is a simple acceleration of the body's electromagnetic field which produces a sympathetic resonance in the target. In the case of humans, this greatly enhances the healing process. Months to days, days to hours." His hands returned to normal. "I have developed a program that simulates this in virtual reality. The enhanced systems made this possible. Commercial systems will not immediately recognize its usage as hostile, giving us time to weaken or penetrate the firewalls and possibly blind the watchtowers."

"For how long?" Overguard asked.

Populus shrugged. "A few minutes. It is hard to be certain."

"Long enough to set the botnet?"

"I believe so."

Mason spoke up. "Nicholson, do you think you're up to it? You have the most information about the systems. Your perceptions will drive the I/O programming."

"I have done it once. I can do it again."

"Good. You and Meeker will..."

"Hold it," Overguard cut in. "I think Janice has done more than enough."

"I can do this, Stephen," Meeker protested.

"I know you can, Janice. It's just that I feel like I've been a bit of a fifth wheel lately." He looked at Mason. "Is there a reason for that?"

"Nothing deliberate," Mason said.

"Then I volunteer."

Mason glanced between them. "What do you think, Populus?"

"Nicholson would be planting the bot. Overguard would be a back-up observer."

Mason nodded. "All right. Nicholson and Overguard go. Tripp, Meeker, and I will go in as far as Populus to safeguard the breach."

"There is something you should all know about Andlat's systems," Populus said. "It is based on a very advanced version of magnetic bubble tech. There is a VR interface to the mainframe patterned on a separate reality, one you have seen hints of inside the VR you took from Azazel. The interface to Andlat will be much more sophisticated than what you have previously experienced, more detailed, and more dangerous." He paused to let that sink in. "What happens to you in there could very well have real physical effects on you here."

"But hasn't that always been true?" Meeker asked. "The enhanced interface often has psychological side effects."

"You do not understand," Jaelon said. "What he means is that what you encounter there can manifest here using the interface as a locator. In other words, if you are not careful The Enemy can follow you back."

"Oh," Meeker breathed.

"All the more reason I should go instead of Janice," Overguard said.

"Yes." Populus turned to Malthusan. "If you and Jaelon would be so kind as to do what is necessary should the occasion arise?"

The Cypriot nodded solemnly.

"What's that mean?" Meeker wanted to know.

Populus grinned. "I will be the finger in the dike, as it were. Should I fail, my colleagues will see to it I do not become an unwilling agent of The Enemy."

"Agent?" Meeker queried. "You mean the feedback..."

"Would displace my consciousness with whatever might get through," Populus finished. "In which case I would become a danger to everyone here."

She looked at Malthusan. "You would kill him?"

"He would already be dead," Malthusan replied. "I would be dispatching an Enemy influence."

"How would you know?" she objected, stunned.

"It would be evident, believe me."

She slipped her arm into Overguard's and put her head

on his shoulder. "My God," she sighed.

Populus began handing out the I/O sets.

"The longer we delay, the less our chance of success," he said. "I advise haste."

Overguard took a set and slipped it over his neck.

"Check your comms," Mason said, tapping his own.

Clicks echoed in his head and Overguard nodded with the others.

"Ready?" Populus said. "Three. Two. One."

* * *

He was standing in an open field facing a wall that ran completely around him at a distance of about 200 feet. It was taller than he could see. The ground looked like concrete. In short order the others appeared soundlessly and looked around.

"I will begin shortly," Populus said. "Mr. Nicholson and Mr. Overguard, you will see an opening appear. Step through it as soon as you can. Remember, I can keep it open for only a few minutes." He extended his hand toward Nicholson. A black box appeared in his palm. "Take this," he said.

Nicholson took the box, which immediately disappeared

into his flesh.

"That is the bot coding," the Greek went on. "When you reach your destination, place your hand on or in the receptacle. The code will transfer after a few seconds. Mr. Overguard will be standing by to pull you out in case of trouble."

"All right," Nicholson said. "What am I looking for?"

"More than likely you will know it when you see it. One thing. Remember, whatever you see or hear in there is tied to the outside world through an interface. That means anything can be considered a threat no matter its appearance. Do not be fooled. Stay alert and vigilant."

They nodded their understanding. Populus turned to Mason and the others. "I will be totally defenseless so long as I am holding the portal open. That means my life is in your hands. Most threats will come through the portal, but there are safeguards that might appear here with us."

"Understood," Mason said.

"What do we use for weapons?" Tripp asked. "Bad language?"

Populus laughed. "I have programmed your interface using the patterns you already established. Hostile presences will trigger the weaponry."

"What patterns?" Meeker asked.

"The ones you were using before we met. I believe you referred to them as game characters."

"Wait, you mean the avatars from the MMORPG?"

"Yes. Are they insufficient?"

They looked at each other worriedly.

"I guess we'll find out soon enough," Tripp said.

"If you are not comfortable with the arrangement, I can work something else..."

"No, there isn't time," Mason said. "Let's just get this done."

"Very well. Here we go."

Overguard watched the Knight place both hands on the wall. Immediately Populus went absolutely still. His hands began to glow, first red then shifting through the colors up the spectrum until they went through violet. A vibration began in the wall that rumbled left and right along its length. It sounded around and behind them, returning to crash back into itself, shattering a section of the wall which fell inward.

He followed Nicholson through quickly.

They found themselves on a sea shore. Looking behind him, he could see Tripp peering at them through a hole in the air.

"Break a leg," Tripp said.

Overguard stepped backward and bumped into Nicholson.

"Sorry," he mumbled.

"Well," Nicholson said. "Where to start?"

The beach spread away from them in either direction. Low hanging clouds hugged the far horizon. It appeared to be late afternoon, judging from the long, dim shadows they cast. The sand climbed into a short grassy meadow which itself sat within a circle of impossibly gnarled gigantic trees. No sound greeted them but the rhythm of the surf. He could see no trails or structures in sight.

"Populus picked a nice empty spot to get into," he said.

"Hope it's not all like this," Nicholson said. "I don't see anywhere to insert the code."

"Guess we go inland."

"Right."

They set off into the meadow toward the trees. With no sign of a trail, they picked a thin area to enter the forest.

"Interesting," Nicholson said as they picked their way through the thin underbrush.

"What's that?"

"That our interface is picking this up at all. I have only a cursory knowledge of Andlat's systems, and everything

Populus said in his explanation was so much magic to me. Janice said she had to get Populus to create a doorway last time she went in with no data."

Overguard considered that. "He said this was based on a separate reality. Maybe he programmed our interface with what he knew of it."

Nicholson grunted, unconvinced. "Maybe."

They pushed on in silence for a few moments without a sign the forest was thinning.

"This is taking too long," Nicholson worried.

As he finished his statement, they broke through suddenly into the open.

They were back on the beach. A little way up they could see their own tracks where they had gone into the clearing.

"What the... ?" Overguard said. "We just walked in a circle?"

"So it would seem," Nicholson said, squinting at the trees. He looked at the ground and raised his hands. "Um. Overguard?"

"Yeah?"

"I think I'm sinking."

"What?"

"A little help?"

He took a step toward Nicholson and felt his foot sink into the sand. He snatched it back, spraying sand on the other man's pant leg. Leaning over, he reached for Nicholson's outstretched hand.

Their hands passed through each other.

"Of course," Nicholson said, bitterly. "VR. We can interact with the environment but not each other." He struggled in vain briefly, only managing to sink in up to his knees.

Overguard glanced around until his eyes lit on some driftwood nearby.

"Hold on," he said.

"Not going anywhere," Nicholson promised.

He tried to pick up the driftwood, but it wouldn't budge. Obviously it was only a part of the background.

"You think they know what's happening?" Nicholson asked.

"Probably not," he replied, casting around for another tool.

"Well, I have Populus' code in me. Think this qualifies as 'you will know it when you see it'?"

A tree branch maybe? he thought. He ran to the nearest one and yanked on a low bough. Nothing happened.

"Hey, Overguard."

"What?" he snapped, trying another branch without success.

"Somebody's coming."

He looked at Nicholson, who pointed. A man in medieval garb was running toward them. Overguard moved to plant himself between Nicholson and the other. He readied himself for trouble, puzzled that the weapons Populus promised didn't appear.

Then he got a good look at who it was coming toward them.

"Martin!" he shouted in relief. "Are you a sight for sore eyes."

"Hello! What are you doing here? And who is your friend?"

"Never mind that. Help me get him out."

"No problem."

Martin reached down and pulled Nicholson bodily up and out of the sand. The men gaped at him in surprise.

"How did you do that?" Overguard asked.

"Do what?"

"Pull him out. I couldn't even touch him."

"Maybe you're not properly interfaced." Martin eyed him narrowly. "How exactly *did* you get here?"

Nicholson stopped him answering.

"Excuse me, but I don't believe we've been introduced."

"Aaorld Maachen is the name. You might know me better as Harold Martin."

"Pleased to meet you. Is there somewhere around here I can clean up? Salt water isn't exactly good for my clothes."

"Certainly. Follow me."

Martin set off up the beach at a pace that had them jogging to keep up. Overguard was confused at Nicholson's attitude toward the man who have saved him, but was glad to see Martin alive. He wanted to ask Nicholson why he'd interrupted, but had to save his breath for the jog.

At last they arrived at a little thatched cottage. It was rough-hewn from native materials. Several crude fishing poles leaned against its walls. A net stretched across a frame near the open front door. Martin ran inside as they arrived. He came out with a pair of pants and a shirt.

"Here," he said, offering them to Nicholson. "They should fit."

"I'm sure they will. I want to thank you for what you did back there."

"It was nothing, really."

"Please." Nicholson extended his hand.

Martin grasped the offered hand and froze. He flickered like a broadcast image, then disappeared.

"What happened to him?" Overguard asked, looking around.

"We need to get to the portal," Nicholson said, heading down the beach. "Let's hope Populus still has it open."

Overguard ran after him. "That wasn't Martin?"

"I don't know who Martin is," Nicholson said between breaths, "but I must not have seen what you did."

"What do you mean?"

"I mean, I saw a woman."

They arrived back at the bit of beach where the portal had been. The gate was gone.

* * *

Nicholson and Overguard had just stepped through the portal when things began to go wrong. Mason and the others suddenly found themselves garbed as their game avatars, weapons at the ready.

Surrounding them appeared four creatures out of nightmare. They were all of a type, humanoid with skin glistening like black leather. Faceless, there was little doubt they had some visual sense, as they kept their fronts toward the group. Mason pulled Meeker behind him.

"Guard Populus," he said, pushing her toward the Greek. "Tripp."

"Here."

"Two and two, left and right, back to Populus."

"Gotcha."

Mason ignored the two nearest Tripp and concentrated on the others. The creatures paced back and forth, watching him move.

"What do you suppose they are?" Tripp asked.

"Not friendly. Some kind of security recon, maybe, sent to investigate the disturbance Populus is generating."

"Why just four?" Meeker asked.

"Four of us, four of them," Tripp chuckled. "Don't jinx it."

The humanoids stopped moving and closed in slowly.

"Orders?" Tripp asked.

Mason quickly ran through the game mechanics, what their avatars were capable of. His own was a fighter, skilled in simple weapons and hand to hand combat. Tripp was less of a fighter and more of a rogue, versed in stealth and intrigue although he was capable of handling himself in a pinch.

Meeker's avatar was the least likely to survive close combat, geared toward the game's magical system, nothing likely to work in this environment. So, they were actually two against four.

"Keep them moving," he said. "If possible, away from Populus."

Tripp crossed his field of vision, trailing one of the humanoids.

"They're not following," he said. "They're targeted one on one, boss."

"Meeker?"

"Yes," came the reply. He could hear the tension in her voice.

"Don't let it touch you."

"No problem. What about Populus? There's one headed for him."

He looked around and saw that one of the humanoids was within a few feet of the Greek.

"Damn!" he said, and launched himself at it.

They collided heavily and went down. Mason rolled back to a fighting stance, and found that all the other humanoids had turned toward him. The fallen one rose and joined its fellows facing him.

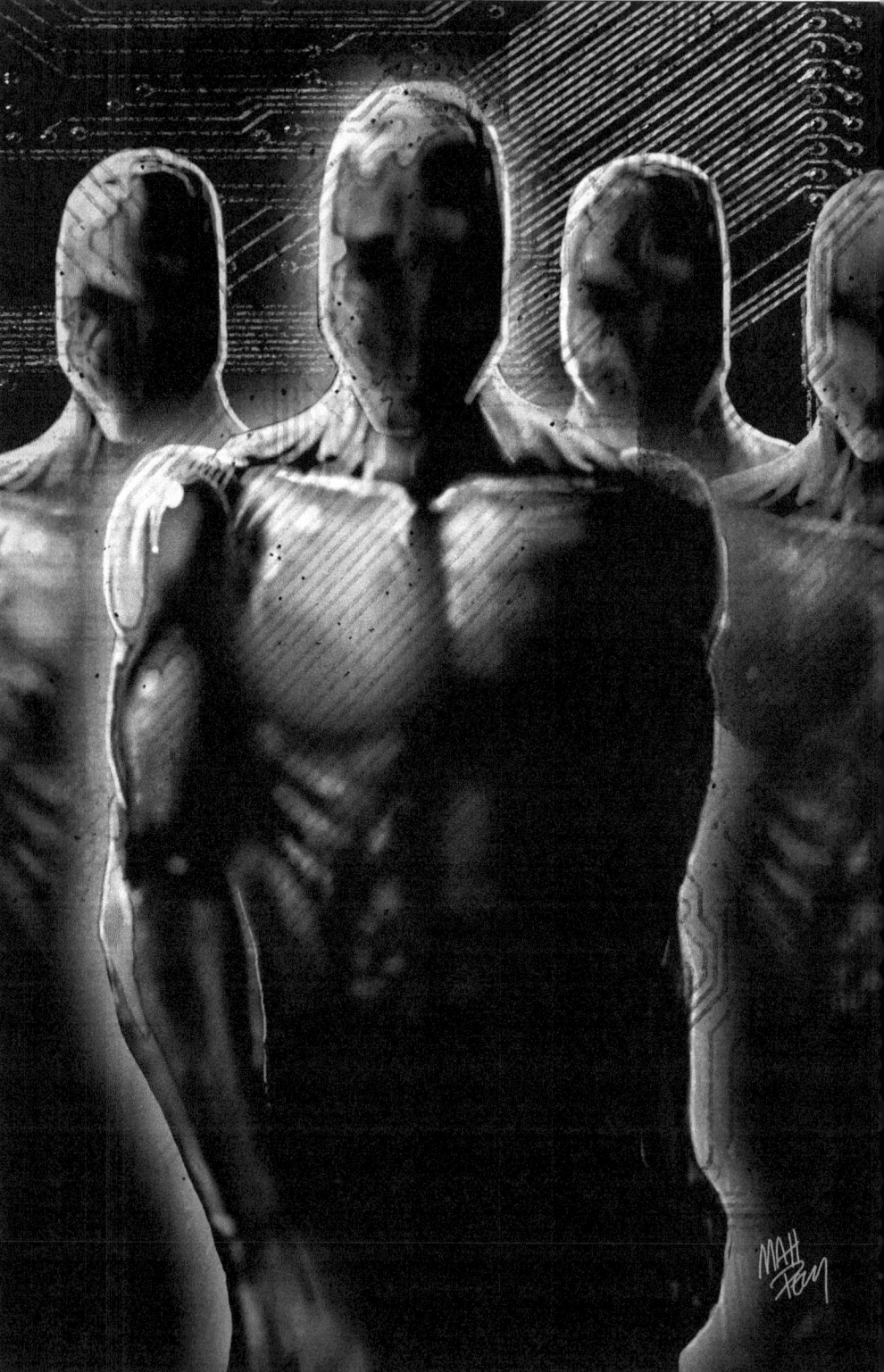

"You got their attention, boss," Tripp said. "Now what?"

The humanoids in unison began to tremble rapidly.

"Uh, I don't like this," Tripp said, backing away from them. "I think we need to go."

A low hum generated by the humanoids' shaking gained volume and frequency.

"Boss," Tripp said. "You hearing this?"

"Meeker, how is Populus?"

"Still not moving. The portal is closing, though."

"What about Nicholson and Overguard?"

"No sign of them."

"Don't think we can wait," Tripp put in.

The hum became a buzz.

"The contact I had with the humanoid is being processed," Mason deduced. "It's just a matter of seconds before we're identified as a threat."

"Then I suggest we leave," Populus said, lowering his hands and turning.

"What about Stephen...and, and Mr. Nicholson?" Meeker asked.

"I am sorry, my dear."

They were back in the cabin. Mason blinked and shook his head to clear the disorientation.

"I apologize for the abrupt transition," Populus said. "It was necessary."

Mason pulled the I/O off. "Can we go back in for them?"

"I would not advise it. Either they have succeeded or failed. We should know soon enough. As for Misters Nicholson and Overguard, I am afraid they will have to shift for themselves."

Meeker threw her I/O at Populus. "Shift for themselves? They're right there!" she shouted, pointing at the men sitting quietly nearby, eyes closed, I/O sets blinking. "Get them out! You got us out. Why can't you get them out?"

Populus held up his hands. "My dear, I..."

"Stop with the 'my dear!' Get them out!"

"I cannot."

That shocked them all. Populus toyed with his I/O and pulled it off.

"They are inside the firewall. The portal is closed. I have no way to pull them out," the Greek explained.

Meeker put her hand to her mouth, tears shining in her eyes.

"Believe me, my... Miss Meeker, if there was any way..." He broke off as Meeker dashed from the cabin.

Everyone left shuffled about for a few moments,

avoiding each others' eyes. They could hear her crying outside, but even Jaelon knew it wasn't the time to intrude.

"What do we know?" Mason finally asked Populus. "Anything?"

The Greek went to the news broadcasts.

"Let us see," Populus said.

* * *

"Okay, now what?"

Overguard scratched his head and looked up and down the beach. Nicholson stood with hands on hips, scanning the place the gate should have been.

"We find another way out," Overguard said.

The other man sighed. "You think? And what would that be?"

"Hold on, now. We're in a VR simulation. A really good one, but it's still a simulation," Overguard said, holding up a finger to make his point. "So, we find a way to log out."

Nicholson gazed at him expectantly. "I'm listening. Populus said you were supposed to be there to pull me out in case of trouble. Well?"

Overguard grit his teeth. Why did he save this man from

the quicksand? Never mind. He would work out the reason for his stupidity later. Right now, they needed to get out of this sim. What had Populus said about emergency disconnects? They were very disorienting and possibly induced nausea. They could be accomplished through visualization, that was it.

"We need to visualize the interface sets, feel them around our necks and pull them away," he told Nicholson. "That should suffice as a log out."

"That's all very nice, but I don't know what they look like."

"What do you mean? You have one on now. How can you not know what it looks like?"

"I didn't look at it that close, okay?" Nicholson snapped. "I'm not into computers."

Overguard snorted. "Fine. Watch me." He imagined the I/O set around his neck and felt it suddenly pressing against his throat.

"Fascinating," Nicholson said, peering at the device.

"Do you think you can duplicate that?"

"I'll try."

"If you can't, you may not be able to get out."

"Why don't they just disconnect us?" Nicholson asked.

"I imagine because doing that could mess with our brains."

Nicholson grunted. He stared out to sea. A band appeared around his neck. He reached, but it vanished just before he curled his fingers around it.

"Damn," he said.

"Keep trying."

Nicholson gave him a hard look, then went back to it.

* * *

The outages spread through the Andlat systems like wildfire. If it weren't for the compartmentalization of its branches, the botnet inserted by the anonymous hackers would have eaten into the entire network and shut the company completely down. As it was, the western branches were down for weeks and the Middle Eastern hubs had to adapt to their lack of support from the central office in New York.

The offices of Andlat Enterprises were spread across the globe, but the nerve center of the entire operation was ensconced in a high security floor of the 130-story Enkeli Building in New York.

Built in the days of steel and glass, before the advent

of more eco-friendly materials, the Enkeli Building was a monument to the opulent and decadent twentieth century, a reminder of a society bent on using every resource available without consideration for the future. It towered over its fellows, edifices already showing their age in contrast to its pristine brilliance. The others were succumbing to disrepair and neglect, but the Enkeli Building, like its master, was constantly kept neat and tidy by an army of sycophants. Like a mad swarm of ants, they bustled on every floor, cleaning, renovating, and maintaining, using materials often especially manufactured just for Andlat Enterprises because the parts were no longer produced commercially.

But even the frantic attentions of those lackeys could not protect Andlat from the ravages of the botnet. As the company suffered, so did its prestige in the eyes of its investors. Andlat stock plunged in every market to all-time lows. In a desperate attempt to avoid bankruptcy, the board shed Catalina Industries and several of its North American branches within twenty-four hours of the cyber attack.

Without fanfare, without the knowledge of more than a dozen people, one of the largest corporations in the world came almost to a complete stop.

* * *

Overguard stretched cramped legs and groaned at the returning circulation. His neck hurt. He pulled the I/O away and turned his head side to side to loosen the stiffness. He looked over at Nicholson, who was pulling off his own set.

Now that they were out, all the questions about him and Janice came thundering back. It was something that needed to be settled.

He looked up to see Janice hovering over him.

"Are you okay?" she asked.

"Fine," he smiled. "We're both fine."

She gave the other man a quick glance, then sat down at his feet. "I'm so glad you're okay," she said softly. She lay her head on his knee.

"Were we gone that long?"

"Long enough for me to worry."

That statement gave him a warm feeling. He stroked her hair. Nicholson walked by, nodding to him. Apparently the man wasn't unfamiliar with gratitude.

But he still didn't like the guy.

EPILOGUE

"It wasn't him, but somebody in their network must have seen him." Overguard crossed his arms. Their report had brought many questions from Populus, mostly about the pseudo-Martin. "If we're going to get him back, we need to get back into Andlat."

"There doesn't seem to be much more we can do," Jaelon said as she gazed at the I/O device she held. "With the central computer damaged, we have no real way to get in."

"Not through the VR, anyway," Populus agreed.

Mason tossed his interface device onto the table. "Well, then, we do it the old-fashioned way."

All eyes turned to him.

"We go after the Director personally," Mason went on.

"Are you out of your mind?" Nicholson objected. "I know him. I know what he can do, the resources he can use. You have a better chance of spitting into a hurricane and staying dry."

Populus snickered at that, then shrugged when Nicholson gave him a dirty look.

"Look, we know he must be in trouble with his own superiors by now," Mason explained. "With the loss of Catalina Industries' main computer and the breakdown in his security, he's as vulnerable as he's ever going to be."

"I don't know," Overguard put in. "Even crippled, he's pretty formidable. Are you sure you want to chance losing this entire cell just to get one Minion?"

"Stephen has a point, Mason," Meeker agreed. "Wouldn't it make more sense to be content with what we've already done? I mean, look, his major operations are shut down, the majority of his infrastructure is in a shambles. How much is enough?"

Mason looked at Malthusan. The Knight took the hint and spoke.

"Azrael is a linchpin," the big man said, ignoring the thrum of the wards at the pronunciation of the name. "If we can unseat him, we remove a key part of The Enemy's hold on humanity. The deception that The Enemy uses to keep mankind under its thumb is based on finances and politics. Those are the avenues we must use to recover mankind. We have to shift the power in those two arenas from The Enemy to The Master. I doubt anyone on the outside will realize what has happened, but the difference will slowly manifest itself over the years.

"The Enemy worked for millennia to gain control and is deeply entrenched. It has taken centuries for us to get this far, but we have much farther to go. We are fighting a battle in a larger war, one that we can still lose in spite of the gains we have made." Malthusan looked at Jaelon. "The three of us were sent to help, to reinforce what you might do, but the direction of that action must come from you."

Silence settled over them as the cell considered their options.

"If you are content with what you have accomplished, we are willing to accept that," Jaelon said. She looked at each of them in turn. "But ask yourselves this: is he hurt enough he cannot recover? Given enough time, could he not regain what he lost?"

Mason watched as each of the others thought about Jaelon's question. Overguard scowled and uncrossed his arms. Meeker chewed on her thumbnail and stared into space. Nicholson sat shaking his head and mumbled something inaudible.

"Wait! There is one thing everyone seems to have

forgotten," Populus stepped suddenly forward to say. His face was ashen and he looked shaken. "Something either we have been blinded against, or conveniently neglect to remember."

The looked at each other and him in confusion.

"Exactly who is he in the Hierarchy?" Populus asked.

A silence settled over them until Jaelon gasped.

"How could we forget?" she stammered.

Meeker sat up, alarmed. "What? What did we forget?"

The truth crashed in on Mason at that moment. How indeed? It was something they should have remembered from the beginning. It made sense, though, that they would forget. If they had recalled the truth, they would never have agreed to work for the Minion.

"Traditionally," Mason said, "Azrael is the name of the Angel of Death."

The wards shivered again.

* * *

The top floor of the Enkeli building consisted of a single office. In that office stood a single desk and chair. No ornamentation graced the walls, not even the seemingly ubiquitous logo emblazoned on every other wall in the building.

The room was as bare, empty, and sparse as the ethics of the man who owned it except for an *Amorphophallus titanum,* better known as a corpse plant, standing in the far corner. The tip of the plant's obscene inflorescence, resembling an eight-foot phallus, tickled the asbestos ceiling tiles. Its odor of rotting flesh usually kept intruders at bay.

Dorian Azrael sat stone still at that lone desk, feet flat on the floor, hands on the desk in front of him, fingers curled into fists. A small pool of blood was forming under those fists, blood that oozed from where his fingernails bit into the flesh. Tiny scarlet rivulets traced their way out of the corners of his eyes to drip from the line of his jaw.

Standing before him, shifting in and out of vision, was a figure that could only be described as hellish. Its only clearly visible traits were the eyes, fiery orbs floating randomly inside its shadowy depths. It might have been humanoid once, might even have been female in the vaguest sense of the word. It was difficult to tell for sure through the miasma of dark swirling around it. A definite smell of lilac hung thick in the air, forlornly attempting to sweeten the stench of rot that rose from the phantom.

Time is short. Your resources are crippled. You have been compromised.

"Your concern is unmerited," Azrael said. "This is something easily handled."

Your continuing failure to control your subordinates has been noted.

The temperature in the room dropped drastically. The blood leaking onto Azrael's face froze.

You will not cause further concern.

"I understand."

There was a growl like distant thunder and the room was suddenly empty except for Dorian Azrael, who sat chewing his lower lip thoughtfully. A dark scowl spread over his features.

The *Amorphophallus titanum* withered and fell over.

ABOUT THE AUTHOR

H. David Blalock has been writing speculative fiction for nearly 40 years. His work has appeared in print and online in over three dozen publications, spanning every format from short stories to novels, non-fiction articles to screenplays. He is also editor of _parABnormal Digest_ for Sam's Dot Publishing.

To find out more visit his website at www.thrankeep.com.

Check out the following pages to see more from

All Seventh Star Press titles available in print and an array of specially priced eBook formats.

Visit www.seventhstarpress.com for further information.

Connect with Seventh Star Press at:
www.seventhstarpress.com
seventhstarpress.blogspot.com
www.facebook.com/seventhstarpress

Epic Urban Fantasy-The Rising Dawn Saga

A shadow falls across the world, and realms beyond, as a war that has raged since the dawn of time itself draws closer to a decisive clash. As groups aligned with a movement called The Convergence speed up their efforts to bring about a global economic and legal order, resistance mounts after the host of a syndicated radio show, Benedict Darwin, discovers the true nature of a virtual reality device that has come into his possession. The Rising Dawn Saga will take you into mythical, supernatural realms as it unfolds, as the most unlikely of individuals rise to confront powers that have existed since before the world began.

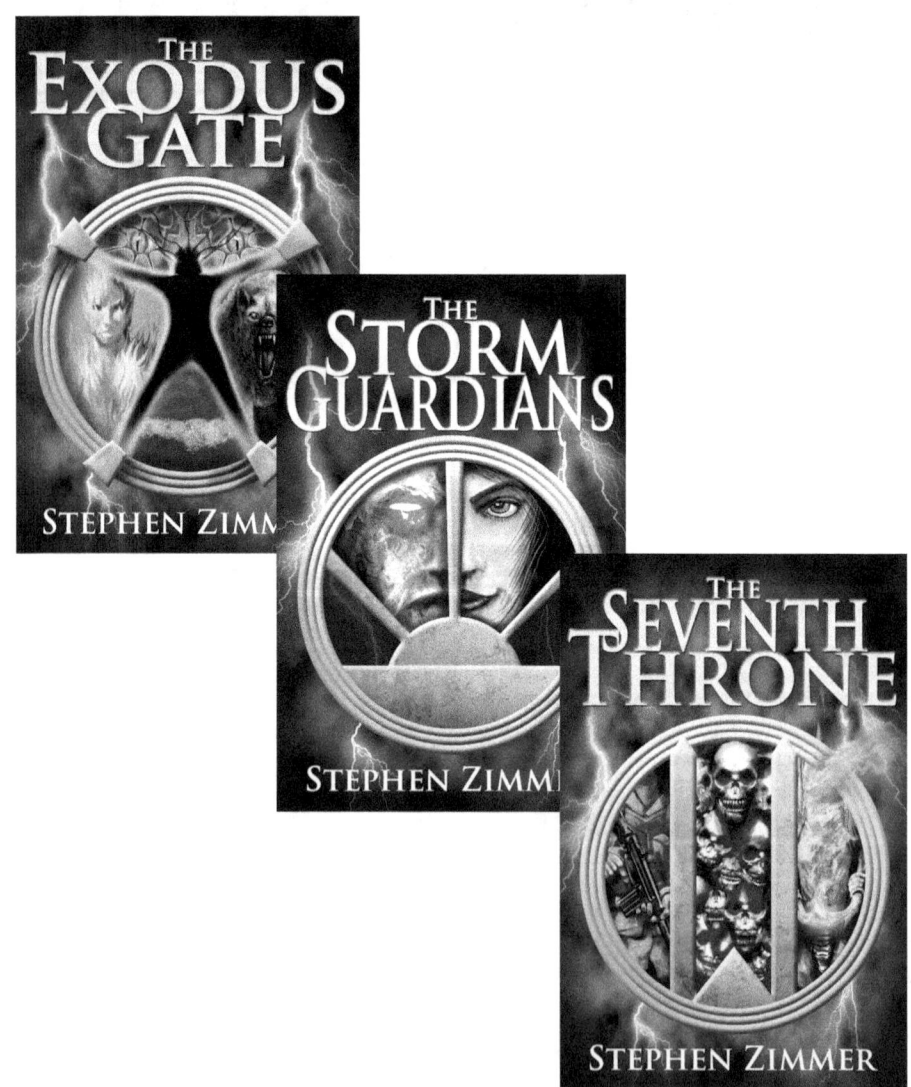

Book One: The Exodus Gate
ISBN: 978-0615267470

"With The Exodus Gate author Stephen Zimmer sets the stage for an adventurous new science fiction fantasy series that is sure to entertain the reader from beginning to end. Zimmer has weaved a tale of fantastic realms populated with exotic creatures. Keep a sharp eye out for this new series."
                                        -Mark Randell, Yellow30 Sci-Fi

"…a book that Fantasy Book Review recommends for lovers of thoughtful-fantasy. It is also a book with an ending that is near-prophetic, written as it was before the world's economic meltdown."
                                        -Fantasy Book Review

Book Two: The Storm Guardians
ISBN: 978-0982565636

"This novel transports me from my bedroom to the edge of an upcoming storm — a battle to be fought by incredible villains and noble heroes of all forms. I love Zimmer's imagination, as each of his creatures play a pivotal role in the bigger picture. Unfortunately, for every auspicious being there is an ominous beast lurking in the shadows. Zimmer's weave of fantasy and religious fables leaves the reader sated"
                                        -Bitten By Books

"The scope of The Storm Guardians is massive, opening up and expanding on the conflict only hinted at in The Exodus Gate. The intrigue and action promised in the first book is fully developed and mercilessly exhibited. The Storm Guardians is a non-stop thriller that lives up to the promise of The Exodus Gate and points at an even more amazing denouement in the final book of the series. Once again, Zimmer has used his command of cinematic imagery to give us a spectacular vision of war both heavenly and hellish. Two thumbs up on this one."
                                        -Pure Reason Book Review

Book Three: The Seventh Throne
ISBN: 978-0983740247

NOW AVAILABLE!

Now Available!
Michael West's Aquatic Tale of Terror!
Book One of The Legacy of the Gods Series

Trade Paperback ISBN: 9781937929954

eBook ISBN: 9781937929831

Man no longer worships the old gods; forgotten and forsaken, they have become nothing more than myth and legend. But all that is about to change. After the ruins of a vast, ancient civilization are discovered on the ocean floor, Coast Guard officers find a series of derelict ships drifting in the current–high-priced yachts and leaking fishing boats, all ransacked, splattered in blood, their crews missing and presumed dead.

And that's just the beginning.

Vacationing artist Larry Neuhaus has just witnessed a gruesome shark attack, a young couple torn apart right before his eyes ... at least, he thinks it was a shark. And when one of these victims turns out to be the only son of Roger Hays, the most powerful man in the country, things go from bad to worse. Now, to stop the carnage, Larry and his new-found friends must work together to unravel a mystery as old as time, and face an enemy as dark as the ocean depths.